DAWN OF DAYS

A NEW DAWN™ BOOK FOUR

AMY HOPKINS

MICHAEL ANDERLE

DAWN OF DAYS

From Amy

*To everyone, ever, who has had to work
on their birthday.*

From Michael

*To Family, Friends and
Those Who Love To Read.
May We All Enjoy Grace
To Live The Life We AreCalled.*

PROLOGUE

Donna stared into the fading pinpricks of red as they dwindled and winked out. Blood dripped down her arm, sliding from the knife to her elbow and dripping into the dirt below.

She wiped the blood from the blade and slipped it into its sheath before throwing the remnant back into a lifeless heap. A smile touched her lips.

"I *did* warn you, dear," she said.

Her eyes turned down, and a frown marred her face as she noticed the mess. Casually, she reached up and ripped her dress, splitting the shoulder seam and yanking her sleeve off. She balled it up and wiped her arm before tossing it on the body in front of her.

Donna turned away. The morning sun cast a long shadow in front of her, and she watched it as her eyes took on a glow of their own, turning white as a flawless pearl.

A mumbled word escaped her lips as her shadow changed. It stretched taller, thinning to give her the figure of a lithe young woman. Then, it widened, her neck disappearing in folds of cloth.

Finally, a long staff sprouted from her hand.

Her small smile turned into a grin—not on her own face, but the false image she wore. Donna looked down and brushed off her new white robes.

The ashen staff she carried had the weight and balance of a real one, and the blue of her dress matched her memory of the one she had seen on the Mystic Master.

"Finally," Donna said, looking about. "It's time for the Master to return to her Temple." A throaty laugh bounced through the forest. "They won't know what hit them."

CHAPTER ONE

A remnant charged at Marcus, and he aimed his rifle, pulling the trigger.

Click.

"Dammit!" he yelled. The close-growing trees in that part of the Madlands suddenly seemed to loom overhead, despite the dappled sunlight shining through the patchy winter foliage.

Marcus tried the weapon again, then slapped it hard. A third pull still yielded no blast from the weapon. The remnant before him laughed and crouched low, ready to attack.

Julianne swung her staff, feeling it vibrate as it thunked against the remnant's skull. The brittle bone exploded, showering blood all over her clothes.

Marcus twisted the rifle behind his back, fumbling to attach it to his belt.

"Leave it," Julianne said. "Unless you're so soft you've forgotten how to fight without it?"

"Soft?" Marcus called. He slid his sword out with a *zing* and took the hand off a nearby attacker, then spun to meet a second. That one dropped dead to the ground a moment later. "I'm not soft!"

"Duck!" Julianne called as the one-handed remnant stuck its head up behind Marcus. "Bad move, buddy," she said to the remnant as Marcus threw himself down to avoid her next strike.

Staff met face, and teeth sprayed across the ground. The remnant howled in pain.

"I ge' yoo, bith!" it screamed.

"Sorry?" Marcus said, a hand cupped behind his ear. "What was that? I can't understand you… no teeth, and all." He slashed upwards, piercing the remnant's belly and spilling long, slippery strands of intestine all over the ground.

The dead remnant crumpled, falling back as Marcus pushed it away from him with the toe of his boot.

Artemis lurched up from his huddled position to lean over and vomit. He emptied his stomach, and sat back down.

Marcus cocked an eye at him, then shrugged. "Yeah. It does smell pretty bad, doesn't it?"

Just the very mention of it made Artemis retch again.

"Marcus!" Julianne chided, shaking her head. She passed Artemis her water, wincing when he looked at the glob of flesh stuck to the side and leaned over again. "Oops. Sorry. Maybe we should head back to the river we passed earlier."

Artemis pulled himself to his feet and lurched off back along the path without a word. Grabbing the reins two of the horses, Marcus followed.

Julianne eyed Cloud Dancer. The horse stared back as if daring her to try and mount while still covered in blood and innards. "Fine," Julianne said. "We'll walk."

"You know," Marcus said, tying the horses to a tree and pulling off his shirt. "There *are* less messy weapons you could use."

"What, and give up my staff?" Julianne said, dipping the white stick into the water and letting the gentle waves wash the stains away. She made sure to stay downstream from Artemis as he splashed water on his pale face.

Marcus shrugged. "It's your staff or your pretty blue pants."

Julianne snorted. "My pants are fine, nothing a good soak and a scrub won't fix."

She looked down, wondering if it was worth trying to clean them now. Blood, both fresh and old, had saturated the fabric. They were already becoming stiff—it would take hours to clean them out properly. She settled for wiping the worst of the mess off her boots with a clump of grass.

"There must be a spell for that," Artemis mumbled. "It would fall under the physical realm, of course... but if they had a way to target the organic material, and lift it..."

Marcus shook his head as Artemis continued to ramble about the theoretical application of a magic he couldn't cast. "Why is he with us, again?"

"I need him," Julianne said, patiently. "For a time, at least. If we don't transcribe what he's learned, it might be lost forever. And he's learned a *lot*."

"You mean, he hasn't written it all down already?" Marcus griped. He motioned at Artemis's horse, loaded with leather bags that were stuffed not with clothes or personal terms, but piles and piles of parchment.

"You're not taking my work," Artemis snapped, suddenly coming back to the conversation. "You'll get those grubby fingerprints all over it!"

Julianne sighed. "He won't let us touch it without him there. So, we're not only stuck with him, I'll have to fund an escort to get him back when Bastian has the school up and running."

"Rude," Artemis muttered, talking into the stream. "Talking about me like I'm not here."

"Artemis, I spent half the damn trip trying to make conversation with you," Julianne pointed out. "You didn't respond to a thing I said."

"Oh?" Artemis said. He grinned. "My meditation skills finally exceed your chatter!"

Julianne rolled her eyes as she climbed onto Cloud Dancer's back. "I know you love us, Artemis. That grumpy old man persona is all an act."

He snorted, then awkwardly mounted his horse. With Marcus leading, they set off through the Madlands.

CHAPTER TWO

Marcus sat with his rifle across his lap, fiddling with it.

"I thought you were going to ask Jakob to charge it before we left," she chided.

"I did!" Marcus protested. "And I tested it, too, so I know I put it back in properly."

"Maybe he did something to drain it by mistake," Julianne mused.

"There's nothing *to* drain," Marcus said, frowning. He held up the weapon, showing her the empty slot where the stone would normally sit. "The amphorald must have fallen out."

Julianne pressed her lips together. "Marcus, it can't just *fall out*."

He shrugged. "Well, it's not there now. And before you say, 'I told you so', I know using it as a club wasn't the best idea, but *every* now and then it was needed."

Julianne arched an eyebrow.

"Ok, maybe it wasn't needed *that* often. Still, I've got my sword." He grinned, patting the weapon at his side.

"Sure, until you slap a remnant skull with it sideways and bend it out of shape," Julianne pointed out.

"Oh, come on. I only did that once!" he protested.

"I rest my case."

They rode on, enjoying the morning sun that warmed their skin, even as a cool breeze trailed past, raising goosebumps on Julianne's arms.

"It's going to be an early winter," she said.

Marcus nodded in agreement. "Bastian better hurry up and get his school running, if he wants you back for the opening. The roads will be impassable once the heavy snows start."

Julianne laughed. "Do you have *any* idea how much he has to do first? I'll be lucky if he needs me back by *next* winter!"

Marcus shrugged. "Throw up a few walls and a roof, right? It's not that hard."

"He'll need to build the schoolrooms and accommodation for the students that don't live close by. He'll also need kitchens and a dining hall to feed them. He'll need to find teachers, draw up contracts, provide accounting to the Temple and Lord George to show how our investment is being spent." Julianne spread her hands. "It's hard work."

"Ok!" Marcus said, waving her down. "I get the picture. Lots of boring paperwork, and *then* throw up a few walls." He winked.

"You men," Julianne replied. "Always—" she stopped when Marcus jerked up a hand and motioned for her to be silent.

Julianne gently tugged the reins, pulling Cloud to a halt. Behind her, Artemis's horse stopped, too, though more likely because it had taken cues from the other two. The old man could sit a horse alright, but paid far too little attention to guide it far.

"I smell smoke," Marcus whispered. "Jules, are there people ahead?"

Julianne's eyes turned white as she reached out with her mind. She shook her head. "No people, but I can sense remnant, I think."

Remnant minds were hard to feel, noticeable only because of the low buzz Julianne felt instead of the familiarity of a human mind. She tried to narrow down their location and numbers, but the odd sensation was too indistinct.

"They're probably setting up camp," Marcus commented. "We should be, too, but I don't think it's a good idea if there's a horde of them this close."

"I agree." Cloud took a few nervous steps, and Julianne leaned down to pat her neck. "So, let's go clean them out."

"I had to fall for a girl with a death wish," Marcus muttered with a heavy sigh. "Fine. Shall we go now, while we've got the element of surprise? I don't want to give these bastards a chance to organize."

Julianne wheeled Cloud around and slapped her flank.

"I guess that's a yes," Marcus said to Artemis. "You wait here. Back soon." He kicked his horse into a gallop and followed Julianne into the remnant camp.

Artemis watched them go, shaking his head. "And people say *I'm* the crazy one."

Julianne plunged through the bushes and emerged in a circle of remnant. Cloud Dancer reared back, kicking one in the face and pummeling it to the ground as Julianne reached down and smashed another in the side of the head.

Marcus flew through, using his momentum to make a clean swipe at a remnant. Its head jerked to the side, now only attached to its neck by nothing more than some sinewy tendons on its back.

"Three more!" Julianne called, pulling the horse around for another run.

The first kills had happened so fast, the other remnant hadn't had time to react. Now, however, they stood, baring teeth and grabbing nearby rocks to use as weapons. Marcus steadied his horse and gripped his sword tighter.

One drew a rusty spear, raising it at Marcus. He didn't see the big horse behind him plunge forwards. Cloud Dancer smashed the remnant to the ground and stomped on its head, crushing the skull with a wet *splat*.

Marcus had slid off his horse already, and Julianne joined him on the ground, aiming for the ribs of a remnant that reached for Marcus's face.

It was a good strike. Julianne felt the crunch of broken bones and the squelch of damaged flesh. Still, the remnant whirled around to face her, mouth open to show corroded teeth behind scabbed lips.

"You ruined my dinner, fucking whore!" it spat, seemingly unaware of the jagged bone sticking out of its chest, or the blood pouring from the hole.

When it stepped forwards, it winced as it looked down. Seeing the wound only enraged it more. Julianne swung her staff, missing as the remnant ducked at the last minute.

Without waiting, she spun, using the movement of her weapon to propel her around on one foot as the other raised in a kick. Her boot struck the remnant in the chest, pushing it back into the dirt.

"Last words?" she asked, her boot pinning the remnant to the ground.

"Fuck you," came the gasping reply.

Julianne took one hard, well-aimed swing, and the last remnant was dead. "You, too," she said cheerily, leaning on her staff.

"Could you at least *try* to look a little less smug, please?" Marcus asked. "Because if this keeps up, you're going to end up a better fighter than me, and I don't like that."

"Challenging your manhood?" Julianne asked. She sauntered up to him and leaned in close, pouting her lips.

"That would be totally sexy any other day, but you're covered in gore. Again." Marcus stepped back, flicking off a tooth that had somehow landed on his shoulder. "Come on. I'm dying for a hot bath and some clean clothes."

They mounted their horses after Julianne gave Cloud Dancer a stern talking to for trying to shuffle away when she reached for the saddle. "Listen," she said, pulling the mare's head around. "I know it's gross, but the sooner you get me home, the sooner you get a good wash and lots of treats. Ok?"

Pulling herself up, Julianne ignored the horse's disgusted shudder. "I swear, Mathias has been talking to you and putting ideas in your head, horse. Go on, git!" She nudged with her knees, and they slowly walked back to the spot where they had left Artemis.

Marcus looked around, frowning. Artemis's old horse was tied to a limp branch, but the old man was nowhere to be seen.

"It's like herding cats," Marcus said as he dismounted.

A trail of broken branches and flattened grass soon led to Artemis. He leaned on the ruins of a building, sifting through a pile of rubbish. Above him, a spread of crumbling plaster fell from the wall, scattering in the wind.

The building was old—beyond old. Too-smooth walls eroded into cracked rubble, showing it was likely built even before the Madness.

"Artemis?" Julianne called carefully.

He ignored her, picking something out of the pile and holding it up to the light.

"Marcus, that wall…" Julianne said, pointing just as another handful of fine pebbles tumbled out of cracks in the brickwork.

These landed on Artemis, and the old man irritably flicked his head from side to side. He looked up, blinking, as Marcus started creeping towards him.

Artemis looked back towards the ground, discarding the nearly-invisible filament to pick up another. This time, he held it up, grinned, then flicked the end.

"Found one!" he yelled, jumping to his feet.

The fast movement made him teeter, and he grabbed the wall for support. Marcus dashed forwards, yanking Artemis forwards.

The old man fell to the ground with a cry as the ruined structure rumbled, then collapsed in a cloud of dust, sending larger rocks flying out like missiles.

Marcus threw himself over Artemis as Julianne watched, helpless. Without thinking, her magic grabbed for Marcus's mind.

Are you hurt? she sent urgently

There was a pause. She couldn't reach past Marcus's shields without forcing her way past. *Marcus?*

I swear to the Bitch herself, if this man doesn't have some kind of lifesaving information in that thick head of his, I quit. Marcus relaxed his shields, letting Julianne quickly reassure herself he was, indeed, unharmed.

He grunted when Artemis suddenly started struggling beneath him.

"Where is it? You fool, where is it?" the old man cried, scratching at the dirt.

Marcus stood and brushed himself off. "Where's what?" he asked with obvious exhaustion.

"My thread!" Artemis scrambled to his feet and grabbed Marcus by the shoulders. "Do you know how hard they are to find?"

Marcus raised an eyebrow and reached out one hand to pluck something from the bushy beard that had been shoved in his face. "You mean like this one?"

Artemis's eyes lit up, and he grinned, snatching the wire from Marcus and spinning around to examine it. "Yes! I found it!"

Marcus coughed. "*Who* found it?"

Artemis stormed away, calling, "If you hadn't toppled a building on my head, I wouldn't have had to find it a second time, would I?"

Marcus opened his mouth, but Julianne grabbed his arm, shaking her head. *You know you can't win this,* she sent to him.

"Fine," Marcus muttered, and set off through the long grass

after Artemis. "But *you* can deal with him until we get through the Madlands. No—all the way to Craigston!"

Julianne laughed. "Fine, but you owe me."

"I'll give you the world," Marcus said, raising a hand to his forehead dramatically.

"Oh, I'll be taking more than that, thanks," she replied, grinning.

CHAPTER THREE

They set up camp that night, laying out bedrolls but going without a fire. Julianne stripped her clothes off and wrapped them inside out to stifle the dank, coppery smell.

As she noticed Marcus watching, she paused before slipping a fresh shirt over her head. Julianne flicked a glance towards Artemis, to make sure he had his back to her and was still absorbed in whatever project he was working on.

She slowed her movements, reaching one arm above her head before pulling the linen shirt over it. She shimmied the shirt on, then turned her back on him, giving him a perfect view of her ass as she stepped into a fresh pair of underwear.

As she pulled them up, then stood for a moment, shirt brushing the backs of her legs, she heard footsteps behind her. Marcus's stubbly face grazed her shoulder as he nibbled her ear.

"You're gonna make me pay for the Artemis thing, aren't you?" he asked in a rough, low voice.

"I just showed you my naked butt, and you're thinking about Artemis?" she said, turning around to slap his arm.

He pulled her closer. "Only because if I forget he's here, even for a moment, he might get a shock when he turns around and sees me—"

"Marcus?" Artemis called. "Where did you put my pack?"

Marcus growled and let Julianne go. "You should put some pants on, my dear."

"Not like anyone around here will notice either way," she said with a sigh. She bent down to grab her clothes, standing up quickly when Marcus pinched her ass.

"Over there, Artemis," Marcus called, cutting off her protest. He hurried off to help before Artemis could get distracted and wander off into the trees.

Julianne finished dressing and joined Marcus and Artemis near the pile of saddlebags and riding equipment. She shoved the last of her things into her bag, frowning when she touched something hard.

"What's this?" she murmured, pulling out a smooth, round object. It shimmered a strange reflective color that threw off shades of red and orange as she turned it over in the fading light.

"Where did you find it?" Marcus asked, wandering over. "Back at those ruins?"

Julianne shook her head. "In my bag. Artemis?" she called. "Did you pick this up?"

He gave an irritated glance at the ball and shook his head.

"Huh. A gift from someone back in Tahn, maybe?" Marcus suggested.

Julianne hefted it in her hand, chewing her lip. "Can't be. This was the last bag I packed, and I strapped it straight onto Cloud with another bag on top."

Marcus took it from her and tapped it. The solid *thock* gave him no clues as to what it was made from. "Weird. Are you going to keep it?"

"My bags are heavy enough as it is, I don't need to be collecting rocks," she said.

Marcus lowered his voice and said, "Maybe Artemis can keep it with the rest of the rocks in his head."

Julianne whacked his chest hard enough to make him wince. "Don't be mean. Maybe he did pick it up somewhere and just forgot. I wouldn't put it past him."

She put the rock on the ground, and smiled as Marcus handed her a small parcel of food.

"Annie outdid herself this time," he said. "Have a look."

Julianne pulled back the cloth to reveal a small sourdough roll dotted with olives. She took a bite, savoring it before swallowing. "Oh, that's divine!" she murmured.

Marcus pulled her down to sit beside him on a bedroll, while he lit a small lantern.

"What's Artemis doing?" she asked, noticing a small glow surrounding his silhouette.

"Playing with his toys," Marcus said. "Hey, Artemis! Are you coming over to eat, or what?"

"Almost done," he called back. "Just have to... and twist that in, yes... and... haha! It's done!"

He scurried over to them, clutching something in his hands. "Julianne, it works! It *works*!"

"What works, Artemis?" she asked, sidling over on the mat to make room for him to sit.

Artemis collapsed next to her, folding his gangly legs awkwardly. He grabbed her arm.

"Woah, steady on old man," Marcus said, his eyes flashing dangerously.

"Marcus, it's fine. He won't hurt—*OW!*" she yelped as Artemis strapped something onto her forearm.

Julianne yanked her hand back. The gold band was tightly clasped around a white stone, pinching her skin underneath.

"Don't!" Artemis yelled as she tried to wriggle it loose. "That wire is fragile!"

"So is my skin," she snapped, fiddling with the catch. It

wouldn't come undone, but a wet drop ran down her arm from beneath the stone. "How do I get this off? I'm bleeding, Artemis!"

"Of course, you are. If the amphorald worked without a blood connection, we'd have realized its use much sooner, you know." Artemis grabbed Julianne's arm, and she let him dab away the blood.

She stopped struggling and watched him work carefully, cleaning the area without dislodging the awful pinching sensation. "There's a needle in that Bitch-damned thing, isn't there?" she asked warily.

"How else do you think I was going to break the skin?" Artemis asked, shrugging.

Marcus, red-faced and furious, made to stand. Julianne reached out with her free arm and pushed him back down.

"It's just a little blood," she said reassuringly. "I assume there is a purpose to this, Artemis?"

"What? A purpose?" He shook his head roughly. "You think I'd go around stabbing people with needles and hooking them up to amphoralds for no reason?"

"You sneaky bastard," Marcus hissed. "Thief! You stole my amphorald, didn't you?"

He reached one hand out to grab Artemis, but Julianne swatted him away.

"I only *borrowed* it," Artemis grumbled. "But don't think you're getting it back. Pah, wasting good magic on a stick that goes *boom*." He looked at Julianne. "Go on, try it!"

Julianne sighed. "Artemis, you haven't told me what it is, yet?"

"Yes, I—oh. I didn't, did I?" He frowned, wracking his brain to try and remember.

"Let's pretend you didn't," Julianne said gently. She shuffled around to turn her back to Marcus, who had a snarl on his face and, quite possibly, murder in his eyes.

"Reach out to Bastian," Artemis said. "Or, did I give it to Danil? Which one is the rude one?" Artemis asked.

Julianne rolled her eyes. "Artemis, you had months to sort them out. Danil's the one you didn't like."

"Ah. Then I gave it to Bastian. Go on, mind-speak to him." Artemis waited, eyes wide.

Shaking her head, Julianne tried. Bastian was two days ride away, a distance far out of range of any—

Julianne, is that you? It really works!

She jerked back in shock. "Bastian?" she said. Then, realizing she had spoken it aloud, she repeated it in her mind. *Bastian? Where are you?*

In the hall. Julianne fancied he was wearing a smug grin by the tone of his thoughts. *I'm guessing you're halfway through the Madlands by now?*

A little farther, she answered. *But, Bastian—how?* She loaded the question with all her wonder and disbelief.

She felt the mental equivalent of a shrug. *Ask Artemis. He's the mad genius.*

"Artemis, what is this? How does it work, and can I only speak to Bastian? What about—"

"*Stop!* Stop talking. You're talking too much, and it's making my head hurt. Like him." Artemis scowled and pointed at Marcus.

"I saved your ass today, old man," Marcus reminded him. His face twitched as he struggled to stay mad, but curiosity got the better of him. "What is it, Jules?"

"I spoke to Bastian," she said. "He's in the hall—back at Tahn!"

"Wow." Marcus rocked back to lean on his elbows. "Maybe that is better than a rif—boom stick. I'm calling it a boomstick from now on. Sounds *so* much cooler than a rifle."

"Of *course,* it's better," Artemis said distractedly. "I made it. Move your arm," he snapped, giving Julianne's arm an experimental tug. "It should stay in place. It won't need recharging, not like those silly weapons. You can send and receive messages to anyone who has one."

"We can make more?" Julianne asked, eyes alight.

Bastian, did Artemis leave the schematics? she asked.

None needed, Bastian answered immediately. *He just said the amphorald has to touch your blood, or be linked to it by something conductive. I'm guessing he was right. You know, seeing as I can hear you.*

She could hear the excitement in his voice.

"See if you can read his mind," Artemis said.

Julianne reached out, but couldn't feel anything. She shook her head.

"As I thought." Artemis dug a small book out of his pocket and began scribbling in it. "Messages, but not control or invasive thoughts. That makes it relatively safe, I suppose."

"Safe?" Julianne asked, suddenly wary. She immediately ran a mental check for signs of strain, or fatigue. She felt fine.

"Well, I thought it was 'safe' to show Rogan that spell, didn't I? And look what happened!" He squinted. "You don't think this could be used for bad, do you?"

Julianne bit her lip. "Only as much as it could be used for good. And we've got them now. If it's as simple as you say, it was only a matter of time before someone figured it out."

Artemis slumped in relief. "I'm not telling anyone else. Only you and Bastian know. Oh... and him." He narrowed his eyes at Marcus suspiciously.

"Don't worry," Marcus said. "I can't use it, and I won't tell anyone."

Artemis continued to scribble notes while muttering, "Can't use it, my ass. Stubborn fool. Still, probably safer if he didn't. Bastard's oath, that man with magic? The world would fall."

"I'm right here, Artemis," Marcus said.

Artemis looked up, surprised. "What? Oh. Was I talking aloud?"

Marcus scowled and pointed two fingers at his own face, then pointed them at Artemis. Artemis just squinted, shrugged, and went back to his notes.

CHAPTER FOUR

Bastian woke early the next morning. He debated reaching out to Julianne through the communication device immediately, then grimaced.

She might be asleep, he realized as he threw on his clothes. *Hell, I still would be if I could.* He rubbed his eyes, yawned, and pulled up his pants before quickly throwing his sheets and blanket into some kind of order.

He picked up the thick ream of paperwork beside his bed and grabbed the empty oil lamp, too. That would need filling for tonight. *Tahn will run out of lamp oil if I keep this up,* Bastian mused.

He and Julianne had talked late into the night, testing Artemis's device. They had sent words, images, and feelings through the device. That seemed to be all it could do—but that in itself was a wonder. It meant Bastian could now communicate with the Temple's Master all the way from Tahn.

And that, he thought, *might just save my skin.*

Bastian?

The whisper brushed against his mind so gently he almost missed it. He grinned, excitement making him shiver.

Julianne! he replied. *I was going to contact you, but I thought you might be asleep.*

Julianne's reply was dour. *Have you heard how loudly Artemis snores? I won't be sleeping until I'm home, he's gone, and we've got a mountain ridge between us as a sound barrier.*

Bastian chuckled, remembering how disruptive Artemis's long, hooked nose could be. *Slip some golden seal in his tea,* he suggested. *Clears it right up.*

Seal? Julianne asked. *That tastes foul. How am I supposed to hide that?*

Bastian sent her a feeling of laughter. *It's Artemis. You could fill his tea with mud, and he wouldn't notice.*

He sensed her agreement and sighed, smiling. Despite the heavy stress he had been under the previous days, it was good to know he would have her nearby, in a sense.

I can feel your worry, Julianne sent. *Is everything ok?*

Surprised, Bastian brought his concentration back to the conversation. When he realized he had been leaking his emotions into the mind link, he lifted a shield and cursed.

To Julianne, he sent, *Nothing. I just have a lot to do. I didn't expect how hard this would all be, but I'll get there.*

He held his breath, waiting for her response.

That's wonderful, Bastian. It was always going to be hard, but I'm glad you have it under control.

The confidence she exuded made him wince with guilt. *Under control, my ass,* he thought, careful to keep *that* tightly behind his shield.

He wondered how to cut the conversation short before she asked for details of what he had been doing, but Julianne saved him the effort.

I have to go, Bastian. She sent a feeling of warmth. *We hope to cross back into safe territory today, but we'll have to move quickly.*

Safe travels. Bastian waited a moment in case she responded again, but his mind stayed empty. Well, for all about twelve seconds.

Hey, you're up! Danil sounded far too cheery for such an early hour.

I am, Bastian replied suspiciously. *Why?*

Polly has stuff to do today, so she's left me alone for breakfast, Danil sent. *Do you know how hard it is to eat when you can't see your food?*

Bastian sighed. *Alright. I'll come and feed you.*

He picked a few pieces of parchment out of his pile, along with a pen, tucking them into a satchel. He carefully piled the rest of the paperwork on a table downstairs, placing a glistening, red-hued stone on them for safety.

Wonder where that came from, he wondered. *Gift from one of the villagers, I guess. Either way, it'll come in handy.*

He locked the door behind him and headed off to join Danil. Bastian had taken a cottage nearby after being chased out of Annie's dining room one too many times for littering it with paperwork.

"I really thought building a school would be a grand, adventurous task," he muttered. "Didn't know it would kill me this way. Death by parchmentcuts."

He waved at the few people he passed on the street, shivering in the cold air. The sun hadn't yet crested the mountains to warm the town.

"You need someone to warm your bed, Mystic," Tansy teased.

Bastian blushed, grinning. "I'm headed to Danil's. Polly's not there, but I bet the place is still roasting. Those two have enough heat to cook a whole hog between their sheets."

Tansy clapped a hand to her mouth in pretend shock. "Why, Bastian! I didn't know you had it in you."

He forced a wink and watched her go, face flaming. He had always been comfortable joking around with Garrett, Marcus, and Danil, but making racy comments to a girl in a catsuit? That was a different story entirely.

"I'm going to have to clean up my mouth once I'm principal of a school," he murmured. He shivered again, this time from the weight of that title. *I'm going to be running a school!*

Despite the troubles he had encountered, the thought still brought a smile to his lips.

"Glad to see someone's mood has improved," Danil commented as Bastian pushed open his door.

"Sorry," Bastian said. "I have been a bit of a prick lately, haven't I?"

"Damn right, you have." Danil motioned to the woodstove, already fired up.

A pot sat on top, bubbling away. When Bastian checked it, he realized it was almost empty.

"I want eggs," Danil explained. "But I can't see the timer. Of all the stupid things to ruin breakfast…"

Bastian laughed, filling the pot with a jug. "You've been pampered in the Temple for too long. All those little apprentices running to do your errands, so you'd tip them off about who to bet against when the card games started."

"Yeah," Danil said, leaning his chin on his hand. "I haven't had a good card game in months!"

"Danil," Bastian said, waiting for the water to reheat. "You're a mystic. You can't lose!"

"And don't the villagers know it. As soon as they realized, they kicked me out and never let me play again!" Danil shook his head sadly.

After dropping a few eggs into the boiling water, Bastian flipped the little glass timer over. As he watched the grains fall, he imagined each one represented one of the many things on his plate.

He pictured a tiny image of himself beneath the growing pile at the bottom.

"Someone's feeling fatalistic today," Danil commented. "Everything ok?"

Bastian sighed. "The money Lord George and the Temple have pledged won't cover the school for a month, let alone a year." He fished the eggs out, hissing when he burnt a finger.

He shoved one plate in front of Danil, then plonked the other down next to his papers. "By the time I pay for timber and labor, then order all the books and pens, it'll be almost gone."

"Where are you getting these costs? Surely, the Tahn residents won't rip you off." Danil carefully tapped his egg, breaking the shell. He started peeling it, dropping little bits of shell onto a napkin beside him.

"Tahn still has to rebuild," Bastian said. "I can't ask them to take this on."

Danil snorted. "My friend, I know you're a bit green, but… do you know anything about economics? If you take the work outside of the town, they'll hate you!"

Bastian froze, staring. "Hate me?" he asked, nerves fluttering in his gut.

"A contract like that?" Danil said. "Well, ok. They won't *hate* you, but they'll be disappointed. Bastian, that kind of work can bring *real* money into a town. And prestige. They'll have built the famous Eastern Temple School!"

Bastian choked. "You named my school?" he asked.

Danil shrugged. "No. But it's as good a name as any." He bit into his egg, sucking in air to cool his tongue as hot yolk ran into his mouth. "*Bitch*, that's still hot."

Bastian put his own egg onto a roll, using a fork to squash it down. "Look, even if I ask Francis and a few of the boys to help, they won't do it for free, nor should they. I'm still in over my head, and I can't even bring myself to admit it to Julianne."

"Well then," Danil said, once he had downed a glass of water. "It's a good thing she's gone. You won't have to talk to her for months!" A shadow crossed his face, despite his flippant tone, and the corners of his mouth pulled down. "Pain in the ass, she is. Bitch's oath, I miss her."

Bastian winced. When Artemis had given him the communication bracelet, he had assumed Danil would have one as well. As not only Julianne's best friend, but a mystic who outranked Bastian by an order of magnitude, there was no way that Bastain should have accepted the device instead of Danil.

"That's not *entirely* true..." Bastian said, bracing himself for Danil's outrage.

CHAPTER FIVE

Bette grabbed the slip of paper off the boy and unrolled it, eyes widening as she read.

"Mathias said it was urgent," he panted.

"Damn straight it was," she said, grabbing her sword. "Guards! Four with me. Jarv, pull in a few to replace them. I don't want the town left unprotected while I'm gone."

"What's that?" Garrett called from the bottom step of the lookout post. "There's been another one?"

"Aye," said Bette, hurrying down as her soldiers scrambled to follow. "Remnant again, they said."

Garrett huffed. "*They said.* They wouldn't know a bloody remnant if it bit 'em in the arse. Any casualties?"

Bette nodded. "Two traders. Four still alive. They're still out there," she said, voice flat. "Ye coming with me?"

"Aye," he said, hurrying over to the gates as four horses trotted over, saddled but unattended. Garrett grabbed one, grateful for the druid's foresight. "Do ye wanna wait fer another horse?" he asked.

Bette shook her head. "We don't know how long ago the first letter was sent. We might already be too late."

Garrett pulled himself up, Bette mounting barely a moment later. She wheeled the horse around.

"Sharne, Carey, with me. Sorry, Mack, ye'll have ta stay," Bette said. "But get three more men and prepare ta ride out if ye see the flare."

Mack saluted. "Yes, Captain." Then, he grinned. "If you all get eaten, that leaves me in charge, right?"

"That's the biggest incentive I have right now fer stayin' alive," she replied before kicking her horse.

"Fair enough!" Mack yelled as the team galloped away.

Sharne nudged her horse faster to catch up to Bette. "How far out are they?" she called.

"The message said they're near the Wolf's Head," Bette said, watching for smoke.

She didn't really expect to see it—though remnant would often burn a campsite or town after an attack and cook the bodies, the small band rumored to be plundering the Muirian countryside hadn't been acting like typical remnant.

Though Bette would reserve judgement until she saw them herself, she thought Garrett's theory that they were really bandits *posing* as remnant might well be correct.

They rode hard and soon, the well-worn trail to Muir curled around, and the Wolf's Head came into view. Named for an ancient, crumbling statue at the edge of it, the seemingly random clump of forest stood alone in the flat fields around it.

She knew it was often used as a campsite due to the pond in the center clearing that bubbled with clean water from an underground stream—and that meant it would be the perfect place for the terrified traders to take refuge.

The namesake stone carving of an oversized wolf peeked through the trees, one ear now broken away and the once-pointed nose dulled with age. It had once been a majestic figure, but now it was little more than moss-covered rock.

Bette called the horses to a halt and slipped off, drawing her sword. "Easy, now," she murmured to the horse as she gently looped the reins over a soft, immature branch.

If spooked, the horse would simply pull away from the branch and run. Bette would rather she bolt than be massacred by remnant—or bandits—because she was tied too tightly to escape.

Carey and Sharne go left; Garrett, go right, Bette instructed with silent hand signals before pushing through the first line of trees. She heard sobbing, the sound winding through the trees from somewhere up ahead.

The clearing was right ahead. Peeking through foliage, Bette could see a woman's back, shuddering while she cried. To one side, an old man with a grey, drawn face and to the other, two younger men, with thick beards and dismal expressions.

"Susie, keep your noise down," one of the younger men hissed. "You'll bring the savages back."

That made her stop, though the shuddering continued. Bette caught sight of Carey and signaled for him to stay hidden. She couldn't see Garrett or Sharne, but hoped at least one of them would do the same, in case she had misjudged the situation.

Bette stepped out of the trees, carefully keeping her hands up so the group could see them.

The two younger men jumped forwards, fists balled. "Who are you?" The one on the left barked.

"Yer the traders that sent fer help?" Bette asked. "I'm from Tahn, sent ta keep ye safe until the Muir soldiers come ta get ye."

"It's ok," the woman said. "She's not one of *them.*" She spat the last word, eyes blazing.

"Do ye mind if I ask yer name?" Bette carefully sat on a fallen log, positioned so she could watch all four of them.

"I'm Susie," the woman said, then gestured to each of the men. "He's Bart, and that's Stanley. We hired them for *protection.*" She hissed the words, her voice dripping with venom. "My father's name is Edward."

Hearing his name, the old man's eyes flicked to Bette. "The

ones she won't tell you are Eddie and Carney, my sons. You'll find them on the road back there." His eyes fell. "Carney's the one without a head."

"Can ye tell me what happened?" Bette asked softly.

Susie let out a fresh sob and pressed a hand to her mouth.

"Remnant," Stanley said in a gruff voice. "They jumped us on the road. We fought, but were protecting these two when the others fell."

"You were hired to protect *all* of us," Susie sobbed. "You damn cowards."

Bart snarled, but Stanley just sighed. "Anyway, we managed to barter for our lives."

"Barter?" Bette asked, suspicions flaring.

"Yes," Susie said. "All our food, our coins, my jewelry and the case of silver spice bottles."

"A remnant doesn't barter," Bette said flatly, trying to bite down on her frustration.

"Are you calling us liars?" Bart growled. "They were remnant. All black around the eyes, blood on their faces. The beasts didn't talk, of course, just grunts and snarls. They attacked, killing the brothers and then herding us in here."

"They took the trader's things and left," Stanley finished. He shifted his glance to the old man. "We were hired to protect them from bandits, not the cursed."

"And what do ye think a bunch o' dirty remnant are goin' ta do with a handful of shiny rocks and pretty metals?" Bette asked. "Ye fool. They were *men*. Oh, aye, I don't doubt they painted their faces to look like a remnant, but the real beasties? Ye wouldn't be left ta tell the tale."

Bette gestured for the others to come out. Her three companions emerged from the trees, and Garrett saluted. "The stand is clear. No one about except for this lot."

"It was remnant, I tell you!" Susie insisted.

Bette leaned towards her. "Have ye ever seen one before today?" She asked in a low voice.

Susie shook her head.

"Did ye look them in the eyes?"

Susie jerked her head in a nod. "One. He stared me down, eyes as blue as the ice in his heart."

Bette sighed. "A true remnant has eyes of red—like a mystic or a druid, but a different color."

Susie swallowed, hard.

Bette continued. "They're not like the stories. They talk, alright. Call ye a bitch and a whore, and boss each other around all fierce. They're cunning, if they're not bright in other ways, but all they care about is the hunt."

Susie swallowed. "The hunt?"

Bette nodded. "They kill fer the blood lust, not fer coins. Once they have a taste of it, they'll fight and kill and bite and stab until they're dead. Ye can't reason with a remnant, and they have no use fer yer pretty trinkets."

Susie's lips trembled, and her nostrils flared. "But they were remnant. Bart said…" she hiccupped before continuing. "He said that's why they got scared and wouldn't fight back."

Her eyes fell on the pair of hired guards. "Bitch help me, if you let my brothers die because you were pissing your pants over a few painted-up men, I'll kill you myself."

CHAPTER SIX

Patrick's face drew in as he regarded the man kneeling at his feet, hands and ankles trussed together like a pig set for market. The forest around them was quiet, but Patrick knew the rest of his comrades would be watching.

He sighed, a deep and painful ache tightening his chest as the air deflated his proud posture.

"Please," Leeds begged. "I swear, I was defending myself."

"You engaged those two." Patrick spat on the ground beside him. "You know my rules—we don't kill. We're not bandits. I'm sorry, Leeds. I can't let this go."

Leeds snorted a rough, huffing laugh. "We're not? Could have fooled me. Why should I lay my life down for them? None of them came to our aid when we needed them."

Patrick shrugged. Leeds told the truth, but it didn't matter. He had pledged to get his men out of this mess, to provide for them. His methods were unsavory, but it was all he had. All he had asked was that there be no killing.

Though technically under the protection of Lord Garvenor, their protector had refused to give them soldiers or food to help them establish a new colony when their hemmed-in town had outgrown its spot nestled between two mountains.

When the men had begged re-entry to the town after the first remnant attack, Garvenor had met them at the gate with swords. Claiming they had defaulted on taxes—after nine months struggling on their own, Patrick remembered sourly—he had denied them access and demanded they leave.

Patrick was no leader, but he had done his best to keep his men fed and clothed. It was his idea to dress as the beasts who had attacked them, in hopes they would scare their victims into surrendering and avoid bloodshed.

It had worked, until now.

"We're better than bandits," Patrick said. He forced confidence into his words, though he didn't believe them himself.

"Better?" Leeds laughed again. "At least a bandit goes home with a full belly and gold in his pockets. We're starving, Patrick. Broke and starving."

"But we're not killers," Patrick hissed, guilt clawing his throat.

Leeds had taunted the two young men by the wolf stand. He had acted coy, letting the boys get close enough to think they could land a hit—but Leeds was a fighter, trained by necessity when their tiny settlement was run over by crazed beasts with glowing eyes.

They all were. Those who couldn't fight had died, if not that first night, then soon after. The remnant had swarmed and dogged their heels for days.

"We're not killers?" Leeds asked. He jerked his arms against the tight ropes binding his wrists. "You're gonna let me walk off, then? After all your proud words?"

The dull shine to Leeds' eyes made Patrick swallow a lump in his throat. Leeds knew how this would end.

Patrick glanced away. Then, he flung his axe around in a single swing, feeling it shudder as it contacted flesh and bone.

"We don't kill, Leeds," Patrick said, looking at the headless body sprawled on the dirt. He rubbed one eye with his sleeves. "We're bandits, but we don't kill."

Dinner that night was quail, flavored with some kind of peppery spice that made the men's eyes water. They didn't care, ripping into the two birds with greedy fingers that moved fast over the steaming meat.

Patrick watched his men eat, aware they had noticed his empty plate. They were too hungry to care, stomachs protesting too loud to allow them to offer him a morsel.

He wouldn't have taken it. He had retched twice tonight, once while trying to wash Leeds' blood off his hands, and once when the cook started gutting the birds.

Patrick leaned back on his bedroll and closed his eyes, letting the nightmare he had lived every night for months flit across his eyelids.

A fire, much like this one, had crackled in the center of their makeshift homes. A pot bubbled away, simmering potatoes and beans, carrots and parsnip, scraps of boar, and a scrawny chicken plucked in celebration of their first good harvest.

Maybe the smell had drawn them. Patrick knew it wasn't so, but the alternative was too grim to consider.

For when the remnant had burst upon them, they hadn't been looking at the pot, or the men around it. No, they had been looking over their shoulder, running so fast they had surprised even themselves when they had erupted into the ramshackle town.

No, Patrick thought. *I was wrong, imagining things. Because nothing... nothing could scare remnant enough to send a whole pack running.*

He repeated the lie again and again, finally lulling himself to sleep, only to dream of a thousand remnant all running away from a terrifying beast with glowing red eyes.

CHAPTER SEVEN

Julianne pushed the branches aside, leaning low over her horse, so the foliage didn't slap her in the face. Marcus rode in a similar position ahead, giving her a great view of his ass.

She sent a mental message to him, a combination of image and feeling that let him know what she was thinking.

Would you cut that out? he thought, once he had let her in his head. *You're turning this into a very uncomfortable ride for me. There's not a lot of room on this saddle, you know.*

Julianne chuckled, stretching out her back as the trees cleared enough for her to sit up. Beside them, a tall cliff jutted up from the ground, sobering her immediately.

"Marcus?" she called tentatively.

He reined in his horse, sensing the discomfort in her voice. "What's wrong?"

"This is where we found the remnant," she said.

"What? You found a remnant? Here?" Artemis said. His voice was bland enough that she couldn't tell if he was being facetious.

"She fell," Julianne explained. "From up there. Danil tried to… well, enter her mind, I think."

"Ahh, yes. He told me the story. Quite fascinating, don't you think? After all this time, we didn't know they could send a man mad." Artemis shook his head in wonder, ignoring Julianne's concerned frown.

"Artemis, it was more than illness. Danil was trapped." A shiver went down her back at the memory. "Promise me you won't try it?"

Artemis chuckled. "Oh, I never would. My mind is far too valuable to risk like that, don't you think?"

"Yes, Artemis," Julianne said dryly. "Valuable, indeed."

Marcus slowed his horse, nodding off into the bushes. "You want to go and see, don't you?"

Julianne raised an eyebrow. "How did you guess?"

He smiled. "I know you. And despite *your* mind being far too valuable to risk, I know you won't listen to me about the danger."

Julianne nodded. "You're right, on all counts. Glad you can see it."

She winked at Marcus, then guided their horses off the path and into the brush.

It took a little time to find the body. The flesh had entirely decomposed, fertilizing the nearby soil. Fresh ferns and bright flowers had sprouted in the months that had passed, hiding the bones of the fallen girl.

Marcus helped Julianne clear the brush. Julianne sighed, looking down on the wasted life.

"You weren't really human," Julianne said quietly. "So, I don't know that you would appreciate a human burial. Perhaps this way was best."

She closed her eyes, slipping into a meditation that connected her with the trees and sunlight, the still air and the distant birdcall. An idea came to her.

Julianne stood, and started pulling long grasses and plucking the bright flowers nearby. Marcus joined her, without questioning why they were clearing brush in the middle of an overgrown, abandoned forest.

By the time they had finished, Julianne's cheeks were pink with warmth and a trickle of sweat inched down her back, despite the cold weather. The pile of grasses and flowers was now two feet high.

Julianne carefully draped a layer of grass over the skeletal remains.

"I bid you pass into the arms of our Queen, wherever she may be, for eternal protection and love," Julianne whispered as she worked. "I bid you pass…"

She chanted the words three times. When she finished speaking, she stood, examining her work.

There was now a mound of grass, scattered with flowers. No sign of the dead remnant remained. "They should have been like us," Julianne said. "The magic inside us is what sent them mad, turned them into beasts. If only Ezekiel's efforts had worked for all."

Marcus slid an arm around her shoulder. "They are what they are," he said. "And you gave her a beautiful farewell. Unfortunately, I doubt the other remnant will appreciate it quite so much, and if we're found here—"

"If we're found, we're dead," Julianne said. "Or more likely, *they're* dead. I don't want to ruin another pair of pants, though, so let's go."

They guided their horses back to the path and mounted up. Marcus took the lead, moving at a brisk pace.

"You were quiet back there," Julianne called to Artemis.

"I may not understand the preoccupation with empty flesh-bags, but I do know people get angry when I tell them that," he replied. "I've found it best to stand by and act interested in most cases."

Julianne groaned. "I appreciate your attempt at humoring my efforts," she said diplomatically. "What *do* you think happens to a soul after death?"

Artemis shrugged. "No evidence to suggest any of the

preferred scenarios. It's a mystery I'm afraid I'll have to wait to research."

It hadn't occurred to her he would want to 'research' it, and hoped his statement simply meant he would find out when meeting his end to natural causes, not some ridiculous experiment that might cause his actual, permanent death.

"My interests lay specifically in the realm of magical application," Artemis said. "The afterlife is merely a curiosity I will not have time to invest my intellect in."

"I'm glad of *that*," Julianne muttered.

"Quiet, you two," Marcus hissed, dropping back so he was level with them. "I think we're being followed."

Julianne snapped her mouth shut and strained her ears. Over the steady, muffled thump of hooves on flattened grass, she heard a branch snap.

She lifted her hands to halt her horse, but Marcus grabbed her arm. Shaking his head, he pressed a finger to his lips.

Alright then, she sent to him. *We'll play their little game.*

CHAPTER EIGHT

Bette threw her helmet into the center of the room, shrugged off her jerkin, then slammed it on the table.

"Can ye believe those damn fools? Remnant! Taken in by a bloody ruse and so afraid of some men in face paint that they'd wet their pants before doin' their bloody job!" She thumped down into a chair.

Garrett eased his own armor off and set it down gently. "Aye, it seems like that's the sum of it. But, Bette, if they really thought they were facin' remnant…"

"They were paid ta do a job, Garrett!" she snapped. "If yer too stupid ta know a bandit from a beast, ye shouldn't be promisin' people yer protection!"

He gave a tired nod. "Yer right, me love. But fer all yer angry words about those men, I think ye might just be blamin' yerself even more."

Bette scowled at him, blinking her eyes quickly. Then, she stood up and walked over to punch him in the arm. She stood back, hard-faced and trembling, waiting for his response.

Garrett winced, rubbed his arm and sighed. "Ye *can't* take responsibility for this," he said in the same soft, even tone, as though he wouldn't have a bruise as black as a strangled testicle in the morning. "George never asked ye ta patrol the roads, just our wee town."

Bette sagged, all the fight taken out of her. "He didn't ask, but I should have offered. We knew his army was gutted by that bastard Rogan, and I should have—"

"Ye *should* have done what ye needed to fer Tahn. And ye did! His army might be wounded, but it's still a damn sight bigger than ours." He grabbed her arm. "Ye did the best with what ye had, and that's all anyone can do."

Bette dropped her eyes. "I suppose yer right."

Surprise spread over Garrett's face. "I am?"

"Aye. We did our best, but what we had wasn't enough. So, I'm gonna fix that." Bette stood and made for the door. "Thank ye, ye wee bastard."

As he watched her go, Garrett wondered what he had landed himself in this time. Not that it mattered—he would follow her to the end of the world and beyond.

"Now, I just have to make sure it doesn't kill us," he muttered, deciding that whatever she was up to, he had better find out now rather than later. Or, knowing Bette, she would tell him at the last possible moment.

He jogged outside and almost tripped over Jessop, storming over to Danil's cottage.

Jessop shoved the door open and stormed inside. "You've been avoiding us, mystic!" the old man snapped.

"Ah," Danil said, leaning back and lacing his hands behind his head. "I had hoped you wouldn't notice."

"Those mischief makers in the hall are eating too much. My wife can't keep up with their demands for butter and bread!" Jessop scowled at Danil, waiting for an answer.

Danil simply shrugged. "Jessop, I know Julianne took care of a lot while she was here—and I mean a *lot*—but I'm going in a few weeks and Bastian will be busy with his school."

"So?" Jessop demanded. "You're here now, aren't you?"

Danil sighed and stood. He walked over to the small cottage window and looked out. *Hurry up, Francis,* he thought. He could sense the young man heading his way, but slowly.

"The people of Tahn need to choose someone to lead them. Bastian has told you that—now *I'm* telling you. We won't be here forever, and even if we were? It's not our place." Danil slid a plate of toasted bread over to Jessop as a peace offering.

It worked. Of course, Danil had known it would—he could sense Jessop's gnawing hunger. He had stormed over there in such a rush after his morning conversation with Tessa, he had forgotten to eat.

As Jessop munched begrudgingly, Danil felt the gears turning in the old man's mind. Jessop was no fool.

"You've got someone in mind already, don't you, Danil?" he asked.

Danil shrugged. "Do I? Who would you pick?"

As if on cue, Francis burst into the room. Danil smiled quietly as Jessop stood a little straighter.

"Jessop! Sorry. I didn't expect to see you here. Am I interrupting?" Francis made to go.

Danil grabbed his arm. "Not at all! What's up?"

"I wanted to ask your opinion. Madam Seher's performers have been draining our resources a lot lately. The town won't be able to sustain them indefinitely, not without causing ill will between them and the people of Tahn." Francis paused, twisting his hat between his hands.

"And?" Danil prompted.

"Well... I thought a trade would help. If each of the newcomers can offer their services for two hours each day, that would go a long way to creating some good will. The stronger ones—and the magic users—can help build, or farm."

"And the rest of them?" Jessop asked curiously.

"Well, a couple of their acrobats could go out picking," Francis explained. "They could jump into the trees without even bothering with a ladder. They have at least two seamstresses, and Seher said the man who creates their fancy smoke is a dab hand at creating garden supplements."

"It doesn't take a genius to milk a cow, either," Jessop mused. He caught Danil's gaze on him and understanding dawned.

Jessop looked at Francis with new respect. He nodded slowly. "It's a fine idea, lad. A fine idea." Then, he snatched another piece of Danil's toast and hurried out the door. "Thanks for sorting that out, Francis!"

"Do you think I should?" Francis asked.

"How would you go about it?" Danil asked.

Francis pursed his lips. "I was going to approach the Madam. If she's agreeable—and I think she will be, because I've seen her pushing them to contribute more—then I'll talk to the Tahn folk, see who can do with some help."

Danil nodded. "Good idea to speak with her first. She'll know how to address it with them."

"Then, I thought we could try just having a list of the things that need done. We can pin it up, and let the performers choose what they want to do. Or let Seher delegate, I suppose." Francis sat down with a thump.

Danil noticed his hands still gripping his head, and gently brushed his magic against Francis's mind. "You're just realizing what's happening, aren't you?" he asked with a wide grin.

Francis shook his head quickly.

"Don't deny it. You've been taking charge more and more, ever since Julianne told you to build that bloody wall." Danil sat next to Francis, and took a bite of his toast. It was his last piece and was starting to go cold.

Francis blew out a slow, steadying breath. "That was different. The wall, I mean. Master Julianne gave me that order, so asking people to work on it and provide materials... well, it was for her."

"But now, you're having ideas of your own. *Good* ones. And

people are noticing, and turning to you for advice." Danil finished the toast and washed it down with a swig of goat milk. "Bloody good thing they are, too. I was getting sick of the interruptions."

He stood and walked to the door. "Now, I believe you have a meeting with a certain theatre owner?"

Francis stood and came over to the door. He paused before stepping outside. "You're not… upset?"

Danil snorted. "Francis, we didn't come here to run your damn town. Just save it from those asshole muckers. Now, I suggest you go see Seher. Don't ask permission, mind—just inform her of what you've decided."

Francis turned a little green at the thought of being so assertive with Madam Seher, but dipped his head respectfully and set off towards the hall.

Danil leaned back against the door jam and breathed a satisfied sigh. Footsteps in the hallway brought a tender smile to his lips.

"Danil, did I just overhear you manipulating Francis into becoming the new mayor of Tahn?" Polly asked as she came around the corner.

"Why, yes, Polly. Yes, you did."

She leaned over to peck his cheek. "Fine choice, my dear. And… once he's instated, we'll leave?"

The smile dropped away from his lips, and he looked deep into her eyes—which to Danil meant looking into the reflection of her pretty blue eyes in his darker ones. "Yes, my dear. We'll have our adventure, just as soon as Tahn is in safe hands."

He leaned down and kissed her deeply, wondering how his world had turned so far upside down in such a short time.

CHAPTER NINE

Julianne, Marcus and Artemis continued down the forest path, the silence growing more uncomfortable by the moment. Despite Julianne's mentally-transmitted pleas, Artemis kept craning his head around, trying to see if anyone was behind them.

"I can't see anyone following us," he whispered loudly.

Marcus cringed. He opened his mouth to speak, but was cut off by hollering shrieks as five remnant burst from the trees. Two more jumped down from above, landing just behind Artemis.

His horse reared in fright and bolted forwards, throwing him off. Marcus slapped Cloud Dancer's rump and she took off, while Marcus wheeled around to grab Artemis and haul him up from the ground, gesturing for the old man to hurry.

"Leave the papers!" Marcus yelled.

Artemis ignored him, taking up precious seconds to snatch loose papers from the ground. Finally, tucking them close to his chest, the old man looked up with desperate eyes. "My research!" he wailed, but let Marcus yank him up on the horse.

Artemis slid in behind Marcus and wrapped his arms around the soldier's waist as they took off after the Mystic Master. Marcus could just see Cloud's tail flicking as she ran ahead.

"Maybe we can shake them off," Marcus muttered.

"Ambush!" Artemis yelled.

Marcus gasped as Cloud suddenly stopped, blocking the path with her rump. She tried to turn back, but Marcus's horse almost slammed into her.

"Remnant ahead!" Julianne yelled.

The clatter of weapons and raised voices reminded Marcus there were remnant behind, too. Julianne plunged forwards again, this time with her staff raised high. A scream rang out as Cloud's hooves came down, and another when she turned and kicked out with her back legs.

"Hold on!" Marcus grunted, swinging his mount around to face the oncoming horde.

Four remnant had caught up to them. Marcus dispatched the first with a quick sword thrust.

"Cover your faces!" Artemis yelled. He threw something, and it landed in the midst of the remnant, a trail of fine smoke showing its path.

Two of the remnant glanced at the device, but quickly lost interest. They turned back to Marcus, only to be swallowed by a thick, billowing cloud. The remnant coughed and spluttered, choking on the pungent smoke.

Marcus slid off his horse and quietly stepped inside the hazy barrier. Though his sight was immediately obscured and his eyes watered, the shirt pulled over his mouth let him breath quietly.

He stabbed towards a hacking sound and felt soft resistance. The noise fell silent. Marcus spun towards a cough, then swung his sword out again. Hot splashes of blood sprayed his clothes as intestines spilled over the ground.

Artemis cried out, and Marcus dashed back in time to see a remnant stagger out of the billowing cloud towards the horse. The remnant, still heaving and wheezing, turned as Marcus's boots crunched on the ground.

It wasn't fast enough to avoid the bite of steel. It fell silently when Marcus's sword sliced at the beast's throat.

"Jules?" Marcus cried.

He dashed forwards to find her wrestling with a female remnant. They both clutched Julianne's staff, wrestling with it, each trying to fend the other off. The remnant gnashed yellowed teeth at Julianne's neck.

"Oh, Bitch's breath!" Julianne gasped.

She lashed out with a solid kick, shoving away her attacker as Marcus arrived. He ran towards the remnant.

"Don't you dare!" Julianne yelped.

She swung her staff over her head in a wide sweep, dipping it down, then bringing it back up to connect with the remnant's jaw. Then, she pulled it back and shoved the narrow end into the teetering remnant's chest.

The remnant buckled. Julianne nudged it with her boot, then nodded, satisfied her opponent was down for the count. She turned to shake her head at Marcus.

"You know better than to interrupt me," she said. "I've wanted to use that move since you taught me. She was all lined up for it!"

Marcus laughed. "Guilty as charged," he said. "Next time, I'll stay back until I'm sure you need help."

"What makes you think I will?" Julianne asked.

Marcus shrugged. "You probably won't, but can't I at least *pretend* you need me around?"

"I *do* need you." Julianne grinned. "You always know the best way to get blood stains out of my whites."

The idea of being relegated to Julianne's laundry boy tickled something inside Marcus. He let out a deep belly laugh, loud enough that two crows took fright. They burst out of a nearby tree and shot into the sky, disappearing into the afternoon sun.

"Damn," Marcus said. "It's getting late. I'd hoped to be out of the Madlands by nightfall."

"How far do you think?" Julianne said.

He shrugged. "If we ride hard and don't have to stop again, we'll make it to one of the border camps a little after dark. Are you up for it?"

The ride through had been easier than their first trip together, but it had still been rough.

Julianne regarded him, eyes narrowed. An uneasy feeling prickled down his spine. "Now, Jules," he said, raising his hands defensively. "I've got Artemis riding with me. No crazy—"

"Are you telling me your horse can't handle it?" she asked.

He slumped defeatedly. "At least let me mount, first?"

She gave a short nod. Marcus's ass had barely hit the saddle when she called out again.

"Last one to camp gets to clean my boots!" she yelled as she kicked Cloud Dancer in the ribs. Her horse shot off, leaving Marcus for dead.

"Dammit," he said, urging his horse into a gallop. "I knew she was gonna do that."

Julianne's horse disappeared into the forest ahead, though he could still hear the hoofbeats on the path. Her horse was small, but quick. His was strong, but weighed down by two men.

Shit. Julianne sent the thought with a mental image of the path branching in two directions. *Left?*

What, you don't know? he thought.

Dammit! Frustration leaked through as he caught sight of Cloud's tail, swinging as she danced.

"Yes, left!" he called as he raced past her.

"You dirty cheat!" she yelled.

They shot through the ruins and past a group of startled remnant sitting around a fire. They grunted and yelled, but didn't give chase. As the trail wound through the old building and started to climb upwards, they slowed to allow the horses to choose their path, stepping carefully along the steep mountainside.

Marcus led the way, until Julianne shoved past him when they reached the top.

"Eat my dust, dipshit!" she called, laughing.

"Just don't get lost this time!" he called back as she took a wrong turn, and he ran past her. Cursing, she wheeled Cloud around to give chase.

Marcus spotted the white marker that designated the safe place to stop. He leaned low, kicking his horse and telling Artemis to hold on. Behind him, he could hear Julianne approaching.

He pulled his horse up to jump over a fallen log. As the jolt from the landing slammed his teeth together, something white flashed on the corner of his eye. A tail flicked him as Julianne shot ahead.

Marcus let out a yell of frustration and let the horse slow. She had won.

"Oh, Bitch, that was close," she panted. "And I *really* don't want to spend the afternoon scrubbing clothes again."

Marcus pulled a face at her as he slid off his horse. "You think I do?"

"You don't have a choice," she pointed out. "You lost."

Marcus helped Artemis down. The old man was trembling. "Are you ok Artemis?"

The old man's eyes lit up as a grin spread over his face. "That was wonderful! Shall we do it again tomorrow? Maybe I should ride with Julianne, she goes so much *faster*!"

"Thanks for the moral support," Marcus muttered. He pulled the bags off his horse and threw them on the ground. "Smells like rain," he said as he unrolled one of them. "We'll sleep inside, just in case."

He stuck his head inside the small, stone building and sneezed. Motes of dust swirled in a shaft of sunlight coming through the window and a cupboard in the corner sat ajar. He pulled it open to reveal a ratty old broom and empty, cobwebbed shelves. A moth-eaten blanket sat on the bottom shelf.

"Someone's raided it," he said. "We should hunt for dinner tonight, and leave some of our supplies here."

"Why?" Artemis asked, poking his head in.

"Because it might be us that needs it one day," Marcus said. He pulled out the broom and dragged it on the ground, sending the dust particles into a frenzy. He sneezed again.

Artemis withdrew, leaving Marcus to tidy up the dusty room. It didn't take him long to coax the room into something resembling clean. He set up the bedrolls, his and Julianne's beside each other and Artemis's against the wall of the other room.

Marcus grimaced at the short distance between his mat and the old man's. Artemis would spend the night practically snoring in Marcus's ear.

Julianne popped her head in. "So glad I picked up a domesticated man," she commented. "Margit's going to *adore* you."

Marcus had heard enough about the Temple elder to make him shake in his boots. He knew Margit looked at Julianne like a daughter, and would be fiercely protective over her. He hoped Julianne was right—if Margit didn't like Marcus, he had no doubt she would let him know in the most painful way possible.

"I'll get some water," he said, wiping the dust off his face with his sleeve.

"I've already done it," she said, holding up an old pail. "And Artemis is collecting sticks for the fire."

"Is that a good idea?" Marcus asked. "We don't want him to wander off and get lost... do we?" A hopeful lilt touched his last words.

"I told him you'd catch a rabbit for dinner. He won't go far." She watched his expression flicker between satisfied and disappointed, and thumped his arm. "Oh, come on. He's not *that* bad. Most of the time."

Marcus grinned. "Wait until morning. You think he was loud

in the open air? That little room will echo, his snores will be as loud as a room full of miners chipping stone."

Julianne groaned. "I can't wait to get back to the Temple," she said wistfully.

"Me either," Marcus agreed.

"Marcus, you've never been to the Temple," she reminded him.

Marcus shrugged. "So? Soft beds, warm blankets and the love of my—" He sneezed again, then choked and spluttered, eliciting a giggle from Julianne.

"What, scared of telling me how you feel?" she taunted.

"I just don't want you to go getting a big head." Marcus dropped the broom and caught her in his arms, holding her tenderly.

"Who, me?" she asked, relaxing in his embrace. "I couldn't, not with you making sure I keep my feet on the ground." She leaned into him, tilting her face up for a kiss.

"Is that enough?" Artemis's voice was close enough to make them both jump, and he gave an evil cackle when they jerked apart. "None of that kissy-face rubbish until we're back at the Temple," he said. "You get distracted out here, and it's a remnant that will bite your face off."

Marcus raised an eyebrow. "An expert on the Madlands now, are we?"

"I travelled this way more than once on my own," Artemis said haughtily. "No weapons, no supplies. Made my way through on my own merit."

Marcus gave a low whistle, impressed despite himself.

"Which only proves you're an idiot," Julianne said. "Were you *asking* to be killed? What kind of fool crosses the Madlands alone?"

Artemis scowled at her, then turned his back, flipping his cloak in a fit of irritation. "Get your own damn sticks."

Julianne sighed. "Fine. I'll get the sticks."

"I'll help," Marcus offered.

Julianne shook her head. "No, I'm the one who put him in a bad mood. You see to your snares."

Once Julianne had collected enough for the fire, they sat down to go through their supplies.

Julianne stretched out to warm her toes by the crackling fire, eyeing the sky with unease. Clouds moved overhead, fat with moisture.

"It's a few hours until sundown, which might buy us time to catch some dinner. If we snare a rabbit now, that'll buy us an extra day or so," Marcus said. "But we really need to stop somewhere to stock up before we head into the mountains."

"We *could* stop by Arcadia again. I'd like to see how Amelia dealt with her little problem."

Artemis cleared his throat. "That will take us away from the most direct path. I have a friend with a smallholding on the way, if you'd like to visit there instead?"

Julianne nodded her agreement. "The weather is starting to turn, so the path to the Temple may already be difficult. The faster we get there, the better."

As if to prove her point, a fat raindrop splattered on her nose. Julianne squeaked and grabbed her blanket, diving for cover inside the little hut just as the skies unleashed a downpour.

"Don't you know it's bad luck to predict the weather?" Marcus muttered.

Beside him, Artemis snorted. "That's a construct of the human mind. You're simply more likely to—"

"It's just a figure of speech, Artemis," Marcus said, cutting off the mystic's tirade. He sighed. "There goes our fire, though."

They spent a cold, damp night in the shelter, wriggling to and fro to try and avoid the occasional leak in the flimsy roof. When the first shafts of sunlight peeked through the window, Marcus rolled over to face Julianne.

Her hair, frizzed by the moisture in the air, stood around her face like a fuzzy wreath, glowing in the morning light.

"Marcus?" Julianne cracked an eye open. "Did you just snort at me?"

He grinned. "If you saw your hair, you'd snort, too."

Julianne did snort, then rolled over and flipped the blanket over her head to hide her hair.

"You can't stay under there forever," he taunted. "You'll run out of air."

"Fuck you," came her muffled reply. "Go find me some breakfast, and maybe I'll forgive you."

Marcus rolled off his mat and folded his blanket, then gathered up the bedroll into a tight bundle. As a soldier, the move was second nature to him.

"I'll see if I can restart the fire. Looks like the sky is clear, but it might still be too soggy out to cook anything." He walked out, carrying his bundle.

Julianne pried open her leather packs to check everything inside was dry. She rummaged around her clothes, frowning when her hand grasped something smooth and round.

She withdrew a small, round stone. It was a glossy, reflective color that threw hues of red and ochre as she twisted it in the cool morning light.

"Where'd that come from?" she mused before setting it aside. Pretty as it was, she didn't need any added weight.

She kept digging through the bag, clicking her teeth when she couldn't find what she was looking for.

"Where are my letters?" She mumbled

She had taken a note from Selah with her, a keepsake she rarely travelled without. Alongside it, there would be a letter of introduction from Amelia, and some papers that verified her place as leader of the Mystic Temple. "Huh. I must have put them in with my other papers."

She checked the second bag, assuring herself the pieces of

parchment in there weren't damp, then reluctantly shoved them back in without checking through them. She wet her hands in a small, clean puddle on the floor, smoothed down her hair and gave it a quick comb.

Then, straightening her shoulders, she walked outside. "So, Artemis," she said. "How far to see this friend of yours?"

CHAPTER TEN

Bastian lifted the shiny paperweight and rifled through the stack of documents that lay below. He had already gone through them four times, but had run out of places to look.

"Dammit, where could it be?" he muttered.

Slamming the paperweight back down, he winced as it thunked loudly on the table. Whatever it was made out of, it was sturdy.

He picked it up again and turned it over in his hands. So far, no one had admitted to leaving it in his office. "I don't have time for this," he sighed, and put it back down. He would have to re-write the list of supplies he would need to start building.

Bastian grabbed a satchel and threw an apple in it before setting off to Mary's. The little bar would be empty at this time of day, meaning the food would come out quickly and be fresh and hot.

Not that anyone's ever had a bad meal there, he mused. Mary's had become his second home. Unused to the seclusion of living alone, he often escaped there to work on his monumental project.

Today, he would be meeting with Francis, though he hadn't

divulged why he wanted the young man there when he had asked him.

Bastian arrived early, slipping in behind his favorite table. He waved at Mary.

"Same as usual?" she asked cheerily.

Bastian grinned. "How can I refuse?" he asked, mouth already watering at what lay in store.

Francis arrived at the same time as a giant platter of cheese, cold meat, olives, fruit, and bread arrived. "That's quite a spread," Francis said.

"Oh, I expect to have more visitors than just you," Bastian said. "Anyone who sees me here alone will stop for a few words and a few bites. I learned quickly that if I wanted to eat, I had to order enough for all."

"That must be annoying, having everyone wanting you all the time." Francis frowned, his low voice giving the question more weight than Bastian would have expected.

"Not really," Bastian answered lightly. "It's nice to be wanted."

Francis gave a nervous grin. "Speaking of wanted, what can I do for you?"

"I wanted some help calculating the materials I'll need to start building. I've had quotes from Arcadia, but I wondered, if it's not too much of a drain on Tahn's resources..." Bastian raised his eyes to Francis's, hope glimmering.

"We'd love to help!" Francis exclaimed. "In fact, that will help *me* with another problem I have."

"What's that?" Bastian asked.

Francis explained his idea about asking the theatre troupe to start contributing more to the town's resources, then told him about his meeting with Seher. She had insisted all her members work at least four hours a day—leaving Francis to figure out what to do with the huge workforce.

"Bette needs more men and women to join the guard, at least short term. She wants to send patrols out, wipe out those bandits that have been roaming around," Francis said. "But if she succeeds, she won't need them forever."

"You can't just set them to work around Tahn?" Bastian suggested.

"There just isn't that kind of work to be done! But if I can set the men to logging, we can start up the old sawmill again. I've got seamstresses for curtains and people to cook, build, and haul materials," he said with a grin.

"And I suppose the money will help the local economy?" Bastian said. He hated to admit Danil had been right.

"Money?" Francis chuckled. "After all you've done for us?"

Bastian shrugged. "And you've kept us up, given us places to live. I can't even get Mary to charge me properly for lunch! You'll be paid fairly, or you won't do it."

Francis set his mouth in a line, hesitating. Then, he stuck a hand out. "Fine. It's a deal, then?"

"Deal!" Bastian felt a weight lift. Having the resources locally would make his job so much easier. "Now, I just have to find a site... and recalculate all my material lists. I can't believe I lost that!"

"You've been working hard," Francis said. "Ma always says she can't remember which way her face goes on when she's been putting in too many hours."

"How's Annie?" Bastian asked. "I haven't been out to the farm in weeks."

Francis smiled. "As sharp as ever. Why don't you go see if she knows of a good site for your school? Our Pa was from Muir—Ma used to visit him there before they wed. She would know every inch of land between here and there."

Bastian eyed the spread on the table. "I might just do that." He hailed Mary and packed up his things. "Mary, can you pack this up for me? I'm going to take it up to Annie's."

"About time you went to see her," Mary chided. She rustled under her counter and brought out some waxed cloth and a small crock, and brought it over to Bastian. "Here, use this for the meats and put the cheese in here. You can take that basket by the door if you promise to have it back by sundown."

"I'll return it," Bastian said. "Thank you!" He hurriedly helped her wrap the items and stack them neatly in a basket.

"You can take my horse," Francis said. "I need to go back to the hall, then talk with Garrett about forming a new patrol."

Bastian waved and headed out the door.

"What a day," Francis muttered.

"What's bothering you, love?" Mary asked. She patted his shoulder in a motherly fashion. "Is it a lady?"

Francis laughed. "I wouldn't have time for one of those. No, it's just been a day of… well, revelation, I guess."

"Ah. Well, I wouldn't know too much about that," Mary said. "I just work in the bar and serve beer and food. Too old for excitement, I am."

Francis ducked his head. "Ma'am, you happen to have the best food this side of the Madlands—probably both sides, but I've no desire to go and find out. And your little tavern here might not be as fancy as some of those in Muir, but for us in Tahn, it's the grandest establishment that exists."

Mary swallowed and blinked quickly. When she spoke again, her voice was husky. "Why, Francis, that's the sweetest thing anyone has ever said. I always did know your mother raised you right."

CHAPTER ELEVEN

Julianne closed her eyes and inhaled the scent of fresh grass, letting the swish of a soft breeze through the leaves above mingle with the rhythmic thump of hoofbeats. Bundled up against the crisp breeze, she tipped her face up to catch the feeble warmth from the sun.

"Don't fall asleep up there," Marcus teased. "Or I might tip you off into a stream."

Julianne cracked an eyelid open. "Try it, I dare you."

Marcus laughed and moved his horse over a little, out of arm's reach. "I'm suitably afraid now. What were you thinking about?"

"Meditating," she said.

"About?"

She slid a glance his way. "The whole point of meditating is to *empty* the mind, Marcus."

"So… the answer is nothing?" he asked.

"Yes." Julianne smiled. "And yet, when people ask mystics what they're thinking, they never seem to believe us when we tell them that."

Marcus shrugged. "I guess because for most people, having a head full of bunches of nothing seems…"

"Crazy?" Julianne finished.

Marcus nodded. "Sorry."

"Don't be. We get it all the time."

She slipped back into silence, glad for the rest. Her anxiety levels had been bristling all the way through the Madlands, her magic constantly roaming, seeking the twisted minds of the remnant.

She had hoped that her encounter with them some months ago would have heightened her perception of them, allowing her to sense them from a distance. It had worked, but only sporadically.

Perhaps their minds are as different from each other as they are from ours, she mused. The thought of mentioning it to Artemis just made her feel tired, knowing the question would haunt him until he had found the answer.

Julianne was so wrapped up in her own mind that she almost rode straight past the small cluster of buildings by the road.

"Jules!" Marcus called. "We should stop, see if they can sell us some food." His snares had come up empty and their rations were low, despite deciding against leaving some provisions to top up the safe haven outside the Madlands.

"There's no one—*oh.*" Absent the telltale mental presence, Julianne had assumed the area was deserted, but some washing billowed on a line and an unseen horse whinnied. She focused, but still couldn't find the people that should be around.

Just as she opened her mouth to tell Marcus that, a door slammed shut and a moment later, a pair of curtains were yanked closed.

Whoever is here is shielded, she sent to Marcus. He nodded, and moved his hand to rest on his sword.

"If only my rifle was loaded," he muttered. He couldn't tell if the snort from behind him came from Artemis, or his horse.

A man stepped out from behind a small outbuilding. He was

tall and broad, and a sword hung from one hip. A faded scar traced a line from his scalp to his chin.

"What are you doing here?" he demanded.

Julianne pressed against his shield, but it was strong. *Marcus, I can break through his mental barrier, but it will probably tip him off.*

Don't do it just yet, Marcus thought. *We'll hope they're friendly, but assume they're not. He certainly doesn't look like a man who welcomes visitors.*

"We're travelers, returning to the Heights," Marcus called. "We're just passing through, friend."

"The Heights?" The man's eyes narrowed. "That's what *she* said last time she passed through." He pointed at Julianne.

"I'm sure you're mistaken. I haven't passed this way before," she said coolly.

"Bullshit. You think we don't remember? You tricked us into giving you half our supplies, you traitorous mystic bitch. Adrien was right about your kind."

Julianne opened her mouth to protest, but a noise made her turn. Four more men stood behind them, twisting their hands into complicated movements. As she watched, their eyes turned black.

Arcadians! Just as Julianne harnessed her magic, the ground exploded below her. Cloud Dancer reared, and Julianne slipped to the ground, her trance dissipating. She yanked out her staff, only to have it stripped from her hands. It flew through the air towards one of the magic users. He raised his other hand and squeezed.

"This time you're ours, *whore*."

A hard band tightened across Juliane's throat, cutting off her air. She threw herself against the man's shield and forced through it. She tore at his mind until he collapsed, but the pressure didn't change.

As dark spots floated in her vision, she realized she had attacked the wrong man. Giddiness made her weak as she suffocated, but she shoved her way past it, and dove back into the mind of the man she had attacked.

Through his eyes, she saw Marcus hanging upside down, suspended in the air three feet off the ground. A man nearby clutched his arm, blood dripping through his fingers. Artemis lay on the dirt, face already swelling and beginning to darken into a bruise across his cheekbone.

Julianne took control, taking the Arcadian's body as her own. She drew his sword and lunged at the nearest of his companions, relishing at the feel of the oxygen in his lungs as her own starved for it.

The second Arcadian lunged back. "Take out the bitch, she's got Ronald!"

"Kill her!" another one yelled as a solid force crashed into her skull.

Her tenuous grip on consciousness dissolved and, sending one last, feeble cry for help, Julianne fell into darkness.

CHAPTER TWELVE

Bastian staggered, grabbing onto the table with white knuckles. "Julianne!" he gasped, feeling her cry for help ricochet through his mind. He reached out mentally, but could not find her.

"No." He collapsed into a chair and let out a mighty sob. "Julianne!"

Hands grabbed him, and a sharp sting blossomed into heat when someone slapped him across the face. Bastian shook his head, blinking hard.

"What is it?" Danil demanded. "What happened?"

"She called for help," Bastian said. "Now… she's gone."

"Gone?" Danil snapped. "Is she dead, or ignoring you? So help me, Bastian, if you don't tell me what's—"

"Not dead," Bastian gasped. "Not if the connection is the same as it normally is."

"You're sure?" Danil pressed.

Bastian nodded. "I did my time in the hospital, so I know what it feels like when someone slips away."

"Can you bring her back, Bastian?" Danil's face was white as a sheet and Bastian's arm ached where he gripped it tightly.

Julianne. Bastian sent the message with a push of force to it. *Julianne. Wake up. Wake up, Master.*

"Nothing," he said aloud.

"Try harder," Danil growled.

Clenching his teeth, aware the frustration he felt at Danil's words were governed by his panic over their friend, he closed his eyes.

JULIANNE!

Trapped. Julianne's reply wavered, a paper-thin version of the strong voice Bastian was so used to.

Bastian's eyes shot open as he sucked in a sharp breath. "She's there. Weak, I can barely hear her... but she's there. Stay with me, Julianne," he muttered before reaching for her again.

Julianne, you cried for help and then slipped unconscious. You're not safe.

Safe... came the weak reply. *Safe while I sleep.*

You can't sleep! Bastian sent, making his thoughts as loud as he could

Safe while they... think I'm asleep. Julianne's thoughts became clearer by the second. *They're near, I can hear them.*

What happened? Bastian asked, unwilling to let her stop.

Arcadians. Bad ones. Must be exiles that served Adrien. They attacked, but I wasn't fast enough. Julianne's thoughts faded out for a moment. *I have to break through one of their shields. Bastian, if I don't survive this...*

You will, he sent, more a plea than a statement of fact.

Yes, but if I don't, you must know—Donna was here, masquerading as me. The memories of what had happened were still fragmented, but the Arcadians statement that she had passed through recently and taken their goods was lodged firmly in her mind.

She knew Donna was broken. Not just her will or her emotional health, but her logic. Rogan had treated her so badly, abused her mind so many times, it had shattered into a mere semblance of humanity.

Donna? Bastian asked, a hint of concern in his voice. Not nearly enough concern for what she had said. Julianne realized he thought she had been hallucinating.

She sent him a snippet of memory, of the recognition on the Arcadian's face and the words he had spoken.

Oh, shit! Now Bastian sounded suitably distressed. *Do you think she's gone for the Temple?*

Julianne almost nodded her head, but the act of tensing her neck muscles made her flinch. Her throat ached like fire, and exploded into dagger-sharp pain when she reflexively swallowed.

Her breathing quickened, but she forced it steady. She could not let these men know she was awake. Now that her wits had returned, she paid more attention to her surroundings.

Yes, she sent to Bastian. *Tell Danil. I'll contact you... wait, is it morning or night?*

It's not yet midday, Bastian replied. *Only a few minutes since you sent the cry for help.*

I can't thank you enough for waking me. Julianne wanted to say more, but tears threatened. He had likely saved her life.

Someone grabbed her wrists and bound them roughly. She kept her body limp as they picked her up and heaved her across the back of a horse. She landed face down, managing to make sure her head was turned so she could crack open an eyelid.

"Toby, take care of that soldier. He's no mystic, I guarantee it." The voice came from beside her, rough and low.

"Fine. You really think she's worth the hassle, though?" Toby asked.

"She's their mistress, the head bitch in that cesspit of mind rapists. They'll pay, alright. They'll pay in hard coin, just to watch me slit her throat."

Toby stooped down in front of a body that had fallen in a heap. Julianne's heart leapt into her mouth and without waiting to see if her mind could handle it, she pummeled through Toby's shield.

It wasn't very strong, and he wasn't very smart. Before he could blink, Julianne had full control of his body.

Toby bent down over Marcus, a knife in his hand. Marcus stared back, eyes wide over a tight gag.

"Told you you're getting soft, sweetheart," Toby whispered.

Marcus sucked a breath in through the thick wad of cloth over his face. He didn't move as Toby quickly glanced around, pulled his long, navy sleeve up, then drew the knife over his own arm. Blood welled immediately, pouring out in a steady stream.

Toby rested his arm on Marcus's chest and shoved the knife at him, twisting it so it didn't pierce the skin. As Marcus felt the bonds on his wrists come apart, he let out a convincing cry of pain. Toby pulled his sleeve down and grinned. "Wait until my horse is out of sight, then count to one hundred."

"Do you have any idea how creepy this shit is?" Marcus hissed, laying his head back and closing his eyes. He coughed dramatically before falling still.

Julianne dug around in her host's mind for a moment as Toby walked back to the horses. His face was already pale, but no one noticed the sticky, dark patch running down his sleeve, growing larger by the second.

Toby's eyes flicked over the gang, counting men and noting Artemis hanging over a horse as limp as Julianne was.

"I need to shit," Toby told Alec, their leader. "Whatever Macey fed us last night has turned my guts."

Alec, grunted. "I'm not waiting for you, boy. You can catch up when you're done. If you can't tolerate the food, you can miss your rations next meal.

Toby nodded and walked off, rubbing his guts and letting out a small groan.

Don't worry, Alec, Julianne thought. *Toby won't be needing rations from now on. Then again, neither will you.*

She walked Toby into the bushes and, pushing away his

terror, drew the knife again. She plunged it into his stomach, forcing down any cry of pain he might have made.

Just before he died Julianne slipped away, certain he wouldn't be bothering them again. Alec called out and the horses moved off, leaving a blood-covered Marcus lying by the road.

Julianne's head bounced against the horse's side, bits of saddle poking into her uncomfortably. Her throat was still swollen, making breathing a chore, and it hurt like a bitch with each little jolt.

The road ran straight for a time and Julianne took the time to chip away at the weakest man's shield. She slipped into his consciousness, then grabbed for the information she needed.

Hello, Cedric, she thought. *Sword at your hip. Crossbow in your bag. Dammit, that crossbow could come in handy.*

She turned Cedric's head and saw her limp form draped on a horse in the middle of the procession. Cedric, however, rode at the back.

Stifling a grin both from her face and his, she quietly reached back and drew out the weapon. The path was curved—Marcus had just dropped out of sight. She didn't have long.

Her first shot rang true, lodging in the skull of the man ahead of her. He toppled off his horse, his silent fall marred by the sudden shying of his horse as a foot tangled in the stirrups.

A guard turned around and saw his fallen comrade.

To buy herself another moment, Julianne made the man she controlled call out. "Bandits! Bandits in the grass!"

She aimed the crossbow and yelled again, firing two shots into the grass. Alec yelled and raised his hands. The grass slammed flat to the ground, like a giant sheet of glass had been dropped on it. Julianne shot the crossbow again, and it slammed into his shoulder.

Alec screamed. "The mystic bitch! She's awake!"

He raised a hand and Julianne's air cut off again, but this time, she was prepared… and armed. Well, poor old Cedric was armed.

He fired another round and Alec choked as an arrow sprouted through the bottom of his windpipe.

This time, the spell that choked Julianne vanished before it could strip her consciousness. *Thank the gods old Cedric can aim,* she thought. Julianne lifted her head and slid off the horse, then heard running footsteps behind her. She prepared to confront her next adversary, then grinned when she saw who it was.

"Soft, my ass," Marcus yelled as he leaped into a jump and collided with an Arcadian. A blast of unseen force threw him off, and he rolled away.

Julianne slipped into a trance, ready to break her way into the mind of Marcus's attacker, but something hit her from behind, and she sprawled forwards.

"Fuck the bounty, just kill the bitch!" Someone screamed.

There were three men left—one fighting Marcus, one twisting his hands and the other holding a giant, flaming fireball between his. Julianne gasped, knowing he would throw it before she could break his shield.

He raised the glowing ball, then threw it forwards. Julianne threw herself to the ground, but it sailed past her, towards Marcus. It slammed into the Arcadian's chest, and Marcus jumped back with a yell.

Relief flooded Julianne, her knees shaking at the close call. "Thanks, Artemis!" she yelled as she prepared to take control of their last enemy.

There was no need. Before she could act, he burst into flames. He screamed, running for the bushes before falling to the ground, desperately rolling to put out the fire.

Julianne slipped into his mind—the pain had stripped away his shields, making it easy—and numbed his pain until finally, his brain gave out.

The last Arcadian, the one Artemis held in thrall, bowed. "Never say I didn't contribute to this wretched journey," he said in a gruff voice. "Now, for the sake of the good Queen Bitch, come and untie me before I vomit."

Then, he plunged his knife into his eye and dropped to the ground, convulsing.

Marcus let out a low whistle as Julianne dashed over to a beige horse, stooping to grab a knife from one of the dead on her way. She quickly sawed through the ropes binding his limbs and helped him down.

"Ack, my head's spinning like a drunken farmer," he said. Artemis staggered over to a tree and leaned against it, pale faced and shaking.

"That was one hell of a trick," Marcus said. "I didn't know a mystic could use magic through mind control!"

"Neither did I," Julianne said, her eyes narrowing. "Have you been holding out on me, Artemis?"

He shook his head irritably. "I never share my theories until I'm certain they are correct. Do you think I want to make myself look like a *fool*?"

Marcus opened his mouth, but Julianne elbowed him. *Don't you dare, smartass*, she sent sternly.

Yes, ma'am. Marcus's reply was sarcastic, but held an undertone of downright disappointment.

Artemis glared at Marcus anyway, as if he knew what the soldier was thinking.

"What a waste of life" Julianne murmured. "These men could have done so much... Instead, they chose to plunder and kill." The words triggered a memory and Julianne jumped. "Marcus, we have to hurry. If Donna is at the Temple..."

"Donna? Why would you think that?" Marcus asked.

Julianne huffed impatiently. "You heard Alec say he'd seen me already? His memories showed it to be true. Someone with my face came through this very spot a week ago. She used mental magic to coerce them into handing over some supplies and money."

"No wonder they were pissy," Marcus remarked.

"No, they really were just assholes," Julianne said. She looked around at the horses blocking their way. "Where are our horses?" she asked.

Marcus scowled. "The Arcadians locked them in a barn with a handful of feed and some water. Said they'd come back for them if they lived long enough."

"Bastards," Julianne hissed, sick at the thought of leaving the animals to starve. "What should we do with this lot? Let them loose?"

"My friend will take them," Artemis butted in. "It's really not that far."

Decision made, Julianne grabbed the reins of the two horses closest to her. The injury to her throat still throbbed, but she could breathe properly, and figured the walk would soothe her still jangling senses.

One of the horses leaned over to nuzzle her face. "It's ok, you big beast. We'll leave you somewhere safe, or set you free to run the hills."

He snorted in appreciation as she scratched him under the chin, then gently shoved him away. Julianne caught Marcus's humorous look.

"What?" she asked. "Do I have drool on my shoulder?"

"No," he said with a grin. "I've just never expected you to be so polite to a *horse*."

Julianne rolled her eyes. "Come on. We have to get a move on. I want to get home as fast as I can."

They collected the horses and formed a train, Marcus riding at the front, Julianne and Artemis herding the other animals along from the back. They stuck to the road, and the horses didn't seem to mind. The long grass on other side seemed to dissuade them from wandering off, and the two riders at the back kept them moving forwards.

"Marcus, you see that field of lavender ahead?" Artemis called. "There's a road just beyond it. Turn down there."

Marcus waved to show he had heard.

You can speak to him mentally, Julianne reminded Artemis silently.

He frowned. *I keep being told that's rude. We're only supposed to do that with mystics, aren't we?*

Julianne thought carefully before answering. *Well, mind speaking to someone who isn't expecting it can cause a bit of a shock, and make regular people uncomfortable. And using silent communication in front of others is rude, yes, if they know you're doing it.*

All these bloody rules, Artemis said. *I've tried all my life to adhere to them, but I don't bloody understand a single one.*

A stab of empathy made Julianne reach out to brush his arm. *I know you try,* she sent. *But as much as you fail to understand about people, you do understand magic. You have knowledge most of us could only dream of.*

I do, don't I? Artemis sent, smugly.

For once, his show of ego didn't bother Julianne at all.

CHAPTER THIRTEEN

"She's fine, I swear." Bastian pried Danil's fingers off his arm. "The Arcadians are all dead, and she's picked up a few spare horses to trade for food."

"But are you *sure*?" Danil asked.

Bastian hissed a breath through his teeth. "For the fourth time, Danil, yes! I'm positive. If you ask again, it'll be *you* that's not ok."

Danil blew out a long breath. "Sorry. I just... worry about her."

"As do we all, not that we need to. Danil, between her, Artemis, and Marcus—who doesn't even *have* magic—they took down an entire group of physical mages." Bastian shook his head in wonder. "I knew she could kick ass, but that's still one hell of an effort."

"Selah didn't choose her to lead us because she's pretty."

"Who's pretty?" Polly asked, prancing through the open door and tossing a flowered hat on the table. "I hope I haven't lost you already, my dear." She ducked her head down to give Danil a long kiss, as if to make sure he hadn't forgotten her.

"We were just talking about Julianne," Danil said. "She was attacked on the road."

Polly's hand flew to her mouth. "Oh, no. That's terrible! How many people did she have to kill? I know how much she *hates* that."

Bastian let out a snort. "That's about the sum of it, right, Danil? I think we only worry so much because we forget how damn strong she really is."

Polly swatted Danil's head. "Never doubt that woman, Danil. She'll move mountains if she wants to."

Bastian stood, nodding to Polly respectfully. "I have to go, I'm setting out to look at a potential site for the school, and it's a good hour away on foot."

"Oh, wonderful!" Polly darted over to grab her hat. "May I come? Tahn is wonderful, but Bitch's oath, I'd enjoy the change."

Bastian grinned and offered her an arm. "Of course! I'll tell you all about Danil's time at the Temple on the way."

Danil stood, shoving his chair back with a load squawk. "The hell you will! Bastian, she actually *likes* me. Why would you ruin that?"

Bastian chuckled. "You're welcome to come. Not to stop me, but so you know which stories I've left out."

Snatching his coat, Danil stomped to the door. "Sometimes I wonder why I'm friends with you, traitor."

"So, where exactly are we headed," Polly asked as they walked through town.

"Annie was telling me the road from here to Muir existed since before the Mad times. She said there's another road, leading off to some old ruins. The trees haven't quite taken it over, and the path is already there, if a little overgrown. It sounds exactly like what I need," Bastian said.

Polly narrowed her eyes. "This path… it doesn't happen to be marked by the iron tree, does it?"

"Yeah, Annie said something about that. An old metal pole

that looked like it was struck by lightning?" Bastian nodded. "That's the one."

Polly stopped mid-stride, yanking him back by the arm. Bastian stumbled, grabbing onto Danil for balance.

"What the hell?" he yelped.

"Bastain, you *can't* go there! Not even to look!" Polly's eyes were wide and serious.

Bastian looked at Danil, but his friend looked just as confused as he was. "Why?"

Polly looked up and down the road to check no one was near. She leaned close, and in a low voice, said, "Because it's *haunted!*"

Bastian gaped for a moment, then snapped his mouth shut to keep from smiling. Clearly, Polly was deadly serious.

"Polly, there's no such thing as ghosts," Danil said carefully.

She slapped his arm. "And what makes *you* the expert, then? I've lived in Muir all my life, and we all know about the Iron Tree Ruins." She lowered her voice again and pulled them both in close.

"Legend has it that a bunch of people got lost coming to Muir. They stopped there for shelter in a storm and were attacked by remnant. While the remnant feasted on their bones, the Queen Bitch watched over them and was so mad, she threw down a bolt of magic that split the pole, marking it for eternity. She scared off the remnant, but the ghosts of the poor souls who died have lurked there ever since."

Polly released the two men, and they both stood back, exchanging glances.

"And ever since then," she finished, "No one has survived a night at the Iron Tree Ruins. Especially not in a storm."

Danil narrowed his eyes. "If no one survived, how do you know it's ghosts, and not just a big, hungry mountain lion?"

Polly lifted her chin and turned away. "If you don't believe me, you'll just have to go and get eaten yourself."

"Ok, then," Danil said with a mischievous glance at Bastian.

"Let's go check it out. Polly can wait here, so she can spread the news of our demise if we don't return."

"Like hell!" she squealed.

"Polly, we'll be fine," Bastian reassured her. "It's broad daylight, there's two of us, and we have magic. I promise we'll come back in one piece."

Polly snorted. "You have mind magic, and neither of you can fight for shit. I'm not letting you go alone. Go wait at the gates, and I'll meet you there in a few."

She turned to go, then whirled back around. "And if you leave me behind, Danil, you can eat your damn dinner alone tonight, and I don't care if you won't be able to see it."

Danil groaned. "She really means that. Last time I pissed her off, she ate dinner with me. Every time I went to dip my spoon in my bowl, she closed her eyes. I ended up with more on my face and the table than in my mouth."

Bastian made a choking sound, quickly stifled when Danil turned a mournful look on him.

"I can't believe you'd laugh at that!" Danil complained.

They soon reached the gate and waited patiently for Polly. When she arrived, Danil smirked at Bastian.

"Looks like we've got more company," he said, nudging Bastian.

Bastian just rolled his eyes. "Hi, Tansy," he called. "I take it Polly has enlisted you to help keep us safe from—" he caught Polly's glare and finished weakly "—from whatever we might meet on the road."

"That's right," Tansy said. A knife appeared in her hand from nowhere, and she tossed it in the air, watching it flip three times before she caught it.

"Come on, then," Polly said. "Let's get this over with. I don't want to be caught out there after dark."

She headed off, Tansy by her side. Bastian jumped to follow them, and Danil trailed behind. Soon, though, Bastian walked next to Tansy, following on Polly and Danil's heels as they whispered together, giggling and holding hands.

"Who would have thought," Tansy said, "that rascal Danil would catch a girl like Polly."

"They're a perfect match," Bastian admitted. "Not many people could make Danil toe the line. Julianne could, but—" he stopped, and Tansy laughed.

"But your Master had her eyes on another man? Oh, don't worry," she reassured him. "I won't say anything. And anyway, it looks like he's well and truly over her."

Bastian nodded. "We all knew Danil had feelings for Julianne. He didn't hide it very well, but... he was never like *that*." He jerked his head at the couple ahead, who had stopped for a brief but passionate kiss. "He's completely besotted!"

Tansy sighed. "I know. Isn't it adorable?"

"Adorable? I feel like I need a bath," Bastian said.

Tansy slapped his arm. "Come on, you've never had a girl you couldn't keep your hands off?"

He thought about it and shook his head. "The Temple isn't like the rest of the world. Things are more... flexible there." He coughed, blushing. Despite the fairly open culture inside the Mystic Temple, talking about it outside made him feel like he was twelve again.

"Flexible?" Tansy asked with a wicked grin. "Sounds like a place I could get to like."

She casually leaned forwards into a one-handed somersault, then followed it with a lazy backflip. Bastian clapped.

"I swear, you're made of rubber," he said.

He had watched Tansy travel all of Tahn on her hands, do flips and jumps and impossible twists, and still, each time she performed, it brought a grin to his face.

"You need to get out more," she said, shaking her head. "You're way too easily impressed."

"What's wrong with that?" he asked.

"You'll get taken in," she said pointedly. "You'll be an important person—not that you weren't already, but you'll have a lot more responsibility once this school has opened. You can't afford to get taken in by a few parlor tricks."

"Blueberry friands," Bastian said.

Tansy jerked to a stop. "What?" she said, eyes wide.

"Blueberry friands. You were just thinking it's been ages since you had one. You could almost taste the berries on your tongue."

Tansy narrowed her eyes. "And why were you in my head, stealing my friands?"

Bastian smiled. "I know I'm naive, inexperienced and only of average intelligence." He tapped his head. "But I do have one very big advantage, remember?"

Tansy snorted. "Yeah, until someone comes along who can shield worth half a damn. Which, by the way, you just taught nearly everyone in Tahn to do."

Bastian pouted. "Not *everyone* in Tahn," he protested. "Just… ok, most of them."

Their talk subsided as the road inclined. Bastian's neck prickled with sweat, and heat flushed his face. He would either have to get fitter if he built the school out here, or buy a damn horse.

Tansy seemed unfazed, skipping along beside him and occasionally twirling around. When Polly stopped and pointed ahead, Tansy was the first to run up and see.

She reached a hand out to touch the strange metal pole. It stood straight and tall, the top splitting into four jagged, curling strips.

"It really does look like it was hit by lightning," Bastian said in awe.

"I can see why locals call it the Iron Tree," Danil said.

He shifted his glance to Polly, who stood still, muscles tense. Danil reached his hand out to take hers, but she ignored him.

Wrapping her arms around herself, she jerked her head towards the overgrown trail leading away from the road marker.

"Hurry up. I don't want to be here longer than we have to," she said quietly.

Tansy strode off, her posture confident. Still, Bastian noticed her knife was out again and she fiddled with it, twisting and tossing it in short bursts between putting it away, then pulling it back out to play with.

The walk to the site was short. When the trees cleared to reveal a flat, open space lined by mossy, broken walls, Bastian gasped. It was like pictures he had seen of fallen castles, ancient monstrosities left to weather and crumble through the ages.

The walls cupped a stone floor, broken by age and by the inevitable encroachment of grass blades forcing through, and old tree roots pushing up the wide stones to make the ground ripple like a swelling ocean.

"This is incredible!" Bastian said when he found his voice again.

Danil poked around the edges while Tansy turned a slow circle in the middle of the clearing. Bastian went to look at a more intact section of the ruined building, poking at the foundations and carefully pushing against a wall to test its strength.

Sunlight filtered down to glisten on the grass poking through stone underfoot. A portion of the building remained—a dew-dropped spiderweb crossed an open doorway, and Bastian carefully pulled it free to look inside. A room, the roof worn away years since, held a rotted wooden slab, perhaps an old table top.

In his mind, Bastian could see his school. This would be an office, small and unassuming, but cozy and accessible. By it, a staircase would lead to the upper level, where the classrooms and perhaps some dormitories would be.

Bastian stepped out of the room and followed the edge of the wall around. When he came across a gap, he stepped through. The forest here was sparse, and the white-barked trees reached straight up to the midday sun. A brook babbled noisily, just out of sight.

We can harvest this wood, and reuse the stone, he thought. *If we clear that area, there will be space for gardens, maybe a cottage or two for the teachers to—*

A twig snapped behind him. He froze, ears straining as he slowly turned around. Heart racing, he looked around and realized he had started to wander away from the wall and into the darker part of the forest.

"Hello?" he called timidly. "Polly? Danil, is that you?"

Of course, it won't be Danil, you fool, he cursed himself. *Not alone, anyway.*

It dawned on him. *Sneaky bastard.* Bastian made sure his shields were strong and secure, then stomped back the way he had come.

Certain he would find Danil irking behind one of the thick trees—probably with Polly—he started, a breath catching in his throat when he rounded the crumbling corner and found no one. Bastian raced back to the gap and stuck his head through.

"Bastian, over here!" Danil waved at him from the other side of the fallen building, Polly and Tansy beside him.

Bastian's heart missed a beat. *If he's over there, who was making that noise out here?* He cast one last look at the gloomy forest and jumped back through the wall. *Squirrels,* he thought. *It must be squirrels.*

He joined Danil, doing his best to look merely curious.

"Are you ok?" Danil asked.

"Me?" Bastian couldn't resist a quick glance around at the shadowed corners and drooping foliage. "Sure. I'm fine. What did you find?"

Danil pointed at a dark stain on the stones. "It looks like blood."

Bastian laughed nervously. "That could be anything. There's no such thing as ghosts."

Tansy nodded. "I'm inclined to agree," she said. "But *something* left that mark. Whether it was a hunter or a hungry animal, whatever died was big, and whatever killed it was likely bigger."

Danil nudged him. "I don't want you out here alone, ok? Especially at night."

"You're worse than Julianne," Bastian complained. He withered under Danil's glare. "*Fine.* I'll make sure I bring someone with me."

"Do you still have the magitech blaster that Marcus gave you?" Danil asked.

Bastian shook his head. "Artemis dismantled it to make the communication device. Speaking of which, have we asked Lord George if he can get his hands on an amphorald? It'd be handy if you had one, too."

Danil sighed. "I sent a messenger to him, but he hasn't responded. I was hoping to hear back by yesterday."

Bastian shrugged. "It's ok. Once Julianne is back to the Heights, I'll see if she can send some."

"More than one?" Danil asked.

"Well, Madam Seher uses mental magic. George and Adeline's shielding ability suggests they may be able to learn it, too." Bastian rubbed his bracelet thoughtfully. "Can you even imagine how much that could change our world? Instant communication across entire regions."

Danil smirked. "Instant transport would be better, don't you think? Then we could get our own shiny rocks."

A bird let out a high-pitched screech, and Bastian jumped. Danil noticed—he smirked and flicked his eyebrows up, just for a moment—but he didn't comment.

"Bastian, have you seen enough?" Polly asked. "This place is a ruin. "

"It's..." he looked around. The wide-open space and plentiful resources would be ideal for his needs. They might just need to clear out some noisy wildlife, he decided. "It's perfect."

Polly shuddered. "Well, you won't see me enrolling in it."

"Once it gets cleaned up, you'll change your mind," Bastian reassured her.

Polly grabbed Danil's hand and pulled him towards the trail.

"Bastian, Danil's right," Tansy said quietly. "I don't believe in ghosts either, but it's pretty wild out here. Cats, wolves, bears… you don't want to get caught unawares by any of them."

Bastian sighed and kicked at a stone. "There's just so much to do, and I told Julianne I wanted this school up and running as fast as we can. There's so much magical knowledge here, all different from what we know at home… and yet, so much of the basics are missing."

Tansy nodded. "I know. And I'll help. Anytime you want to come out here, just let me know. But dead men can't build schools, ok?"

She gave him a warm smile and side-checked his hip. "Besides, I might even miss you if you got eaten."

"You would?" Bastian asked, surprised. "I mean, I'd miss you, too, I guess…" he blushed and turned his eyes to the forest as they walked back towards the Iron Tree.

"Gee, you make me feel so wanted," Tansy said with a snort.

"Oh, no, I didn't mean it like that!" Bastian protested.

She laughed. "I know. I'm just teasing. You're as easy to bait as Danil!"

Bastian groaned, but walked back to the main road by her side. "Clearly, the Temple did a horrible job of teaching us about women, despite all the ones that lived there."

"Maybe you could add it to the curriculum," Tansy said with a wink. "Of course, you'll need to learn a lot more about them before you decide."

CHAPTER FOURTEEN

Bette checked her belt, patted her sword, and wiggled her foot, feeling the dagger nestled securely in her boot. A staff was strapped to her saddle beneath a small buckler, and three smoke grenades—courtesy of Madam Seher—were tucked into her saddlebag.

"Ye ready ta go?" she growled.

"Aye, Captain!" Garrett snapped.

Bette rolled her eyes, but didn't rise to his bait. "Francis? Sharne?"

"We're ready," Sharne said with a look at Francis. He nodded, and they set off.

"So," Garrett said once there was some distance between the rearick and the rest of the party. "Why are we bringin' the builder? He's lovely and all, but he's not a fighter."

Bette grinned. "Ye'll see. He's our secret weapon."

"Against a remnant?" Garrett scoffed.

"No," she answered with a chuckle. "Against Lord George."

Garrett's bushy eyebrows shot up to his hairline. "And why would we need a weapon against him?" he asked.

"Shut yer trap and wait 'n see," she scolded. "And treat him with respect."

"Who, George? I always do!" Garrett protested.

"No," Bette said with a grin. "*Francis.*"

Garrett heaved a sigh. "It's politics, ain't it? Ach, I should've guessed. I don't like it, not one bit."

"Yer only job is ta stand around and look pretty, and make sure the only people who die are those pretend remnant we keep hearin' about. That's if we even find 'em, the bloody cowards." Bette spat on the ground, distaste clear on her face.

The morning grew warm, and flies buzzed about, diving into Garrett's beard and zooming away again as he cursed and smacked it.

"Lucky yer not carrying yer sword," Bette remarked. "Or ye'd have chopped off yer nose by now."

"Aye, that's about—who's that?" Garrett pulled his horse up and stood in the stirrups, shading his eyes against the morning sun.

"Looks like Bastian and Tansy. Is that Danil and Polly with them?" Sharne asked.

"Bloody fools," Garrett cursed. "Gone out without an escort. It's not safe; they know that!"

Bette snorted. "Tansy could take ye down in two-point-four seconds, and Polly in not much more than that," she said. "They'll be fine, as long as those two mystics don't get it in their heads ta go off alone."

"Aye. I'll have a chat with the lads tonight," Garrett promised.

"Ye will not!" Bette snapped. "Ye tell 'em to stay tucked up safe at home, and they'll walk straight out ta spite ye. Let me do it. Better yet, I'll talk ta Tansy and Polly, on the quiet, like. They'll set the lads straight."

"Hey there!" Bastian called once he was in earshot. "Out for a walk?"

"We're off ta meet Lord George," Bette explained. When they

got closer, she added, "He's meetin' us on the road, so we can discuss the situation with the bandits."

"Bandits?" Bastian asked, voice cracking.

Bette shook her head. "Ye don't listen to a damn thing I say, do ye?"

"It's alright," Tansy said. "I'll be keeping an eye on our intrepid schoolmaster from now on. He and Danil have both *promised* not to head out this way without a competent guard with them."

"Hey, I don't remember promising that!" Danil yelped. When Polly flattened her lips and crossed her arms, he back-pedaled. "Or maybe I did. Yeah. I definitely did."

"Aye, that's good ta hear," Bette said with a triumphant grin at Garrett. "What're ye doing so far from town anyway?"

"Bastian has found a site for the new school," Danil explained.

"It's not that far," Bastian interjected. "And we'll be able to set up a rest stop and overnight shelter for travelers, to help fund the ongoing costs. Maybe the extra traffic will help to deter bandits, too."

Bette rubbed her chin. "Aye, it just might at that. Do ye mind if I mention it ta Lord George?"

"I'd love it if you did," Bastian said. He gave her directions to the site, and asked her to reassure Lord George he would send a pigeon with more details the next day.

The two small parties farewelled each other and headed in opposite directions.

They stopped for lunch at the stand of trees that the traders had been attacked at. Bette and Garrett scoured the small clump of forest to no avail. Apart from some chewed bones and a discarded flask, there was no evidence of either remnant, or bandits.

"Remnant my cornhole," Garrett muttered.

"That's the fifth time you've said that since we left," Sharne said. "The stories all say they're from the Mads. Rotting faces, growling, spitting. You can't be sure it's not really remnant, can you?"

Bette leaned back. "Ye've seen remnant yerself, lass. Do ye really think those beasts would stop fightin' long enough ta cut a deal? Or deck themselves out with pretty trinkets?"

"Aye, or wander into town ta sell jewels fer coin?" Garrett chimed in. "Trust us, lass, we know what we're on about."

"I didn't say you were wrong," Sharne said, blushing. "I know you both know more than anyone else out here about those monsters."

"And yer right, too," Bette said, voice softening. "It might well be remnant, ones that are just a wee bit different ta the ones we see in the Madlands. That's why we're gonna act as if there 're remnant and bandits and monsters and anythin' else ye can think of."

"Monsters?" Sharne asked, eyes widening.

Bette chuckled. "All I'm sayin' is, ye can never be too careful. Always expect the unexpected, and stay prepared fer the worst. That way, ye'll never be caught with yer pants down. Unless yer Garrett."

"Ahh, ye bitch!" he yelled and Francis burst out laughing. "Don't ye start too, lad, or I'll set a snake on ye next time ye go for a piss."

The story had made the rounds through Tahn a week ago—Garrett, running out of the bushes on a patrol, his pants around his ankles and screaming something about a snake. There actually had been one, a vicious looking serpent with anger management problems.

It seemed Garrett had disturbed it by pissing on its head, no less. When it reared up, threatening to bite the offending source of its disturbance, he'd fled.

"Fuckin' snakes," he muttered now, shoving his food roughly into a bag. "Slimy little bastards need their pointy little teeth rammed into a big old rock."

"Now, Garrett, just because yer scared of a wee—"

"I'm not scared!" Garrett yelled, his voice loud in the quiet clearing. Realizing how silly he looked, he pulled back a little. "I'm just prepared for the worst, is all."

Sharne couldn't hold her giggles in any longer, and their short stop was delayed for a few minutes while she and Bette clutched at each other, laughing themselves into a state of complete uselessness.

Garrett slid a glance to Francis, who was still managing to smother a smile. "Like I said at the time, it's not my fault I've got a cock long enough that snakes see it as a rival."

Francis rolled his eyes and went over to climb on his horse. "And here I thought it was a lady snake, trying to eat her young offspring that emerged from the egg early, too small and withered to survive."

Francis nudged the horse and meandered away, leaving Garrett behind shouting curses and shaking his fist.

The first sign of Lord George's party was the smoke. Black, billowing puffs mushroomed into the air, stopping for a moment before swelling again.

"They're being attacked!" Bette screamed, kicking her horse into a gallop. She raced up the road, Garrett and Francis behind her, Sharne keeping pace next to the rearick Captain.

The small troop ahead looked to have been accosted during a rest stop. Fighters were paired off with attackers in torn clothes and dirty faces. Some had patches of hair missing and others yelled in guttural growls.

"Bandits!" Sharne yelled, riding in to slice one across the shoulder. He howled and clutched the wound, blood pouring down his back.

Bette leaned down to thump one on the head with the hilt of her sword. He folded down into a heap, and the soldier gave her a wide-eyed nod. She recognized the terror in his eyes.

"They're men, ye fool," she said. "Filthy and stupid, but men."

The soldier squinted, trying to process the thought while still in the rush of battle. "They're not..."

"Nay! Ye fools, they're bandits tryin' to trick ye." She grunted and ploughed her horse into one of the bandits who had stood back, holding a bloody sword.

Her horse clobbered him, knocking him to the ground before leaning her full weight on his back. Bette felt the crunch rather than heard it. She pulled her horse to the side and almost fell when a bandit swung at them, making the horse rear back in fright.

Bette jumped from the saddle, rolling once on the ground before coming to her feet. Her sword was already swinging around, ready to take out any unlucky soul who stood too close.

One of the bandits gave her a wicked, snarling grin, showing teeth that had rotted back to little more than stumps.

"Ach, face paint is one thing, ye sack of toad sperm, but those teeth are one step too far."

She lunged forwards, parrying his sword thrust with her own. Metal clanged against metal as he struck again only to meet her defense. Bette swung around, dipping her head under a high swing and slashing for his shins.

The sword bit into his leg, and he squealed like a pig in a snare. "Oh, buck up, ye pussy. A real remnant wouldn't scream like that if the Bastard himself were facin' it down!"

He took a wobbling step, then collapsed on his injured leg. He managed to fend off Bette's first attack, but her second was too fast, and he was too far off balance. Her sword thrust into his belly, then twisted as he shrieked again.

A hard fist across his face cut the noise off immediately. A quick cut to the throat made sure he was out of his screaming misery.

"Come on, lad, that's not how remnant fight. Ye need ta put some anger into it, like this."

Bette twisted around to see Garrett fighting with one of the remaining attackers. The poor man scurried back, almost tripping as Garrett bared his teeth and let out an ear-splitting roar. The rearick tossed his sword aside and jumped, wrapping his arms around the bandit's head.

"Garrett! Stop playing around," Bette yelled. "Just kill the bastard and come give me a hand, aye?"

Bette would later swear she heard something muttered about 'spoiled' and 'fun', but a moment later, the last bandit was on the ground, neck snapped.

"Sharne, Francis. Ye still walkin'?" Bette yelled. The soldiers milled around, dazed, blocking her view.

"Over here!" Sharne called.

Bette pushed her way through the people and saw a pretty carriage slashed with blood and mud. A dead horse lay nearby.

"Ach. Bastards, they shouldn't have killed the wee pony." No matter that the 'wee pony' was a giant draught horse.

"Check the bodies," Bette snapped to a man nearby. "Tie up any that live, and put the worst off outta their misery if ye've got a few ta spare for questionin'."

She approached the carriage and smiled to see Sharne, blood splashed across her coat, talking to Lord George through the window.

"Ye fight well, Sharne?" Bette asked.

Sharne nodded and flicked three fingers up. *Three kills? Aye, she did well, alright,* Bette mused.

"I was just reassuring Lord George that the danger is over, and that the attackers were men, not remnant." Sharne gave the old man a comforting smile.

"She saved my life," Lord George admitted. "One of those beastly men was trying to climb in my window! Can you believe it? He almost had my head when this brave young lady pulled him out and chopped off his head."

"It wasn't all that dramatic," Sharne said. "But he shouldn't have been able to get anywhere near you. What were your men thinking?" she snapped, glaring at the soldiers closest.

Bette shook her head. "I'd ask the same," she said, glowering.

"My fault," George said. "They're new recruits, every last one of them. Well, except Tavish, but he died, unfortunately."

"What the bloody hell 're ye doin' out here with raw recruits?" Bette screeched. She added a belated, "My lord."

George cringed, and Bette immediately felt bad. "My army has been decimated by Rogan," he explained. "The few men I had left that I could trust are protecting the city, trying to undo some of the damage he wrought."

"Aye, I know." She heaved a sigh. "But yer lucky we came along when we did. And at least now, yer men know a false monster when they see one."

Lord George shuddered. "I'm so very glad they weren't real. I don't think my men could have withstood a fight against the mad beasts."

Bette stopped short of pointing out that they very nearly hadn't withstood *this* fight. Instead, she opened the door to George's carriage, so he could step out.

"Now we know they're nothin' but a bunch of piss-eatin' cowards, let's see what they were about, hey?"

She grabbed the nearest man by his hair, hauling up to look at his face. "Aye. This one'ss breathin'. Let's see if we can wake the bloated goat scrotum up."

CHAPTER FIFTEEN

The winding path to the estate belonging to Artemis's friend was shaded by trees, making Julianne's skin chill and dimple. The house at the end—well, a manor, really—stood tall and bright in the afternoon sun.

"Bethany?" Artemis called when they were close. "Bethany!"

The front door swung open and a tall, thin man looked out, shading his eyes. "Who's there?" he called huskily. "We are armed and won't hesitate to defend what's ours."

"You blind goat, Nathan," Artemis hollered, loud enough to make Julianne shield her ear with one hand. "It's me, Art!"

"Mort?" the old man called. "You son of a—"

"*ART!*" Artemis yelled, as Julianne moved away to preserve her hearing. "It's *ARTEMIS*, you deaf old garden slug!"

"Artemis!" The slip of a man hurried down the steps to greet them. "Oh, it's good to see you, friend. Does Bethany know you're here? She'll be so happy to see you!"

He clasped his arms around Artemis, and to Julianne's surprise, the mystic didn't pull away. He was far from relaxed, but seemed to be doing his best to return the gesture as he awkwardly patted Nathan's back.

"Who's Bethany?" Julianne asked, wondering at the strange duo of names.

"My sister," Nathan said. "Yes, our mother was a bit on the reverent side. She thought giving us the names of our Matriarch and her first follower would lead us to do great things." Nathan offered them inside. "I'm afraid we fell a little short of her expectations."

Once the door was securely closed, Nathan reached above his head and yanked on a thin rope. Somewhere above, a bell rang out, low and soft, but deep enough to make the walls hum with energy as it clanged.

Two doors down the end of the hallway opened. A boy and a girl darted out of one, and a heavyset older woman emerged from the other.

"Artemis!" The old woman hurried towards them, her thick body bouncing as she came. She grabbed Artemis's hands and squeezed them, her eyes bright and shining. "You came back!" she breathed.

A smile cracked the old man's face, and he leaned down. Julianne nearly fell over when he reached out and wrapped his arms around her.

"I've missed you, Bethany," he said.

"This is your sister?" Julianne asked politely, hiding a smile.

"Yes, this is Beth. I don't recall you saying who you are, though." Nathan leaned back, waiting.

Artemis winced. "This is Julianne. She is the Master of the Mystic Temple."

Beth gasped. "But... she's not narrow-faced at all, and I don't believe she's snippy! Not one bit, not with a sweet face like that."

Julianne coughed, stifling a laugh at Artemis's stricken look. "I would have been quite young when Artemis left the Temple. I'm sure my face has filled out since then, and I do hope my personality has... mellowed." She avoided the other mystic's gaze. "Though, I was far from being Master, then."

Artemis huffed. "Not like anyone with one eye and half a brain couldn't see you'd succeed him."

Beth clicked her tongue at him. "Whatever your thoughts then, she is your *Master*, Artemis. You must treat her with respect!"

Artemis mumbled an apology and bowed. "I'm sorry, Master."

"It's... fine," Julianne murmured.

Am I dreaming? She sent to Marcus. *Or has Artemis finally flipped a switch and gone mad as a remnant?*

Marcus ignored her, and bowed to Beth. "Beth, it's so wonderful to meet you. Artemis told me all about you!"

"He did?" Beth asked, her face lighting up, just as Artemis let out a wavering "I did?"

"You did," Marcus said with a grin. "That night after... err, after George came to Tahn. The younger one."

Julianne realized he was talking about the battle of Tahn, when she had killed August and sent George running. She had been exhausted that night, but vaguely remembered hearing that half the town—including stodgy old Artemis—had gotten blind, rotten drunk afterwards.

Marcus winked at Julianne, then looked around. "Artemis said you might be able to put us up for the night? Only if it's not a bother. We have horses to trade, if you want them."

"Horses?" Nathan asked. "Well, I won't charge you to stay here. No friend of Artemis would see our door closed to them... but let's see if we can work something out about those horses."

"They weren't exactly procured... ahh, legitimately," Marcus admitted. "Though, I don't imagine the previous owners will be complaining anytime soon."

Unperturbed, Nathan simply nodded. "I see. Well, I don't imagine anyone will notice them here, anyway. Beth, would you see these nice people to one of the spare rooms?"

Beth nodded and grabbed Julianne's hand eagerly. "Come, you can have the top room. It's the prettiest one in the house—well, except my room." Beth stopped, stricken. "Do you want my room? You can have it, if you want. It's just that—"

"No," Julianne interrupted. "No, any room is fine. We're only staying the night."

Julianne let Beth lead her along a narrow corridor and up three flights of stairs. As they went, Julianne kept one eye on where they were going while she slipped into a light trance.

Beth didn't notice the quiet muttering of the spell Julianne cast, or the foreign presence in her mind. Julianne gently examined the older woman, looking for signs of abnormalities.

There, she thought, spotting a channel that was blocked. Beth had likely suffered a head injury, one that had slightly adjusted her otherwise normal development. That explained her childlike manner and odd mannerisms.

It doesn't, however, explain Artemis, Julianne mused. Then again, perhaps it did. Beth was as different as he was, and as likely to be treated as such. Combined with her trusting innocence and complete openness, Julianne could see what might draw him to her.

Julianne could have delved further into Beth's mind to see more of their relationship, but politeness held her back. She would speak to Artemis directly.

"Here it is!" Beth threw a door open to reveal a room so full of pink frills it looked fit to burst. Knitted toys covered the bed and taffeta ribbons hung from the windows, the door knobs, the dresser, and every possible corner or ledge.

"It's… beautiful," Julianne said, summoning a brave smile. *I'm going to have to meditate my ass off to get to sleep in here*, she thought.

"I'm so glad you like it! Is pink your favorite color, too?" Beth asked.

"I prefer white, myself," Julianne said, glad to see a few hints of it through the sea of warm color. "But the two pair nicely together, don't you think?"

"Oh, and Artemis told me that I'd never like you if we met!" Beth scolded.

"I believe I also said you never would," Artemis grumped, coming up behind them. "And I stand by what I said. Give it a week, and you'll be sick of her, too." He narrowed his eyes at Julianne as if daring her to disagree.

"Well, I'm known to be a little stuffy," Julianne admitted. "But I'm trying to be friendlier, thank you, Artemis."

It was true. At the Temple, the weight of responsibility had always weighed on Julianne, but after spending the last months in a strange village with few ties to her normal life, Julianne had realized that her position had turned her into someone who struggled to let her guard down, to relax among friends.

"Yes, well, you could always practice on me, instead of your soldier," he snapped.

Beth turned on him. "Artemis, you apologize right now! It's no wonder people are rude to you when you speak to them like that!"

Julianne was about to protest, but Artemis flushed deep red and nodded. "I'm sorry, Master Julianne," he mumbled. "Now, can we go outside before I piss anyone else off?"

Beth shook her head at his language, but walked back down the corridor. "You can have your old room, Art. I've kept it clean and tidy, just how you like it."

Artemis smiled at her. "Such a sweet girl you are, Beth, and to a cranky old coot like me, too."

She stopped, and he almost ran into her. Beth whirled around, fury in her eyes. "And don't you speak about yourself like that, either, Art. I won't hear it, not in this house! Not after all you did for us!"

"Now, now. Settle yourself, my dear. I can't go saying nice things, or people might believe it. I'll ruin my reputation!" Artemis shuffled around so his back was to Julianne. He clearly didn't want her input on the subject.

"Men! You're all so confusing." Beth threw up her hands and stomped back downstairs, disappearing into the kitchen after pointing Julianne to a small sitting room. "You can rest in there. I'll bring some tea, and we can talk like ladies."

Then, she wagged a finger at Artemis. "And you can go and walk the grounds. I know you like to do that at least once a day."

"I do, at that." Artemis snatched up his hat, which he had left on a table in the hall. "I'll be back for dinner."

Julianne settled down in an oversized chair, admiring the pretty tapestries and a sideboard lined with exquisitely dressed porcelain dolls. Marcus poked his head in the door.

"I've got our things, where do you want them?" he asked.

"Can you leave my papers here?" Julianne asked, remembering she needed to sort them out. "The rest can go in the room at the very top of the stairs. The pink one," she added, eyes wide with meaning.

"The pink one," Marcus muttered as he dropped a pack by her feet. "No problem."

Julianne hoisted the pack onto her lap once he had gone, and began to stack papers onto a small, carved side table.

A young woman walked in, carefully balancing a tray of tea and biscuits. "Ma'am," she said, curtsying deeply. Her eyes darted to the table, and Julianne realized there was nowhere to put the tray.

"I'm so sorry," she said, quickly pulling the stack of paper onto her lap.

"Oh, it's no bother!" the woman said. She hesitated, waiting until the table was clear before sliding the tray onto it. "Is there anything else I can get you?"

"No," Julianne said. "But may I ask your name?"

"My name is Millie, ma'am." Another curtsy, this time deeper.

Before the maid could turn to go, Julianne asked if she had worked for the siblings for very long.

"Work? Oh, ma'am, I don't work here. I live here. I'm just

practicing my manners, see, so I can go and earn me'self a working position in a ladies' house, one day." She paused, eyes darting to the door. "A house that pays, if you know what I mean."

Julianne frowned. "Beth and Nathan don't pay you?"

Millie started, then stammered. "Oh! No, I didn't mean that! No, ma'am. They…" She looked right and left. "Ma'am, you seemed upset at the idea of me not getting my dues. You're… *against* slave-keeping?"

She bit her lip, teeth sinking deep enough that Julianne could already see the marks it was leaving.

"No man, woman, or child will be subjected to it in my presence," Julianne said, her voice strong. "I've fought against it before, and I will again."

Millie slumped in relief, staggering over to a chair and collapsing into it. "Thank you, ma'am. You see, we're not to talk about it with strangers—you know, in case they want to take us back."

Julianne's mind scrambled to put the pieces of Millie's disjointed story together. "So, you were a slave? But you're not anymore?"

Millie nodded. "Nathan came and slipped me out on the quiet. My master was… oh, ma'am, I didn't mind the work, but the beatings!" Tears brimmed in her eyes. "And I guess my leaving was the catalyst, because a little while after that, we got news of Arcadia and the goings on, and all sudden-like, four more of the girls and two boys I worked with were at our door!"

"They ran?" Julianne asked, drawn in by the girl's story.

"They killed him," Millie whispered. Color drained from her face. "Oh, ma'am, please don't tell!"

Julianne smiled and shook her head. "If he kept slaves and beat them, he'll get no sympathy from me," Julianne reassured her. "Truth be told, I was part of those 'goings on' at Arcadia. I fought with the rebels who overthrew the nobility."

Millie jumped to her feet and ran over, kneeling at Julianne's knee. "Truly? Oh, ma'am, you're a hero, truly you are!"

Julianne laughed. "No, the real heroes are still there, as far as I know. I helped a little, as did Marcus, but the real heroes are the people just like you, people who were treated worse than dirt and still found the strength to rise up and fight back."

A tear snuck down Millie's face. "Oh, ma'am. Ma'am, you don't know what a difference this news makes! I can go home, to my family in Arcadia!"

Sudden fear struck Julianne like ice. "Millie… were your family from the boulevard?"

She nodded eagerly. "Yes, ma'am. They sent me to work for the crooked lord, but he took me as a slave instead. Never sent a single coin back to them, I bet."

It was Julianne's turn to sink her teeth into her lip. "Millie, I don't know your family, but I must tell you… not everyone survived."

Millie's breath caught in a gasp. Then, she nodded. "If they're dead, they died for a cause, ma'am, and I'll honor them any way I can."

Julianne sighed in relief. Millie was strong and would survive no matter what, she realized. Still, a helping hand wouldn't hurt.

"If you plan to go back, I can give you a letter of recommendation. Here, pass me that writing table, and I'll do it right now." Julianne dug in her pack and pulled out a fine pen, then rifled through the stack on her lap to find something to write on.

"To whom it may concern," Julianne spoke aloud as she wrote. "It is my pleasure to recommend to you, Millie of—wait, does this estate have a name?" Julianne lifted the pen, careful not to smudge what she had written so far.

"Yes, ma'am. The Aeternitatem Estate."

"Why would it be anything else?" Julianne muttered, as she wrote it down. "Her fine manners, strong spirit, and unflinching generosity will be a boon to any employer. Signed faithfully, Julianne, Master of the Mystic Temple."

Tears now streamed down Millie's face, and she wiped it with a sleeve, carefully taking Julianne's letter between pinched fingers. "I can't thank you enough," she said, her voice strong despite her watering eyes.

"It's nothing, really," Julianne said. "Arcadia could do well with more people like you. I have a friend there, Amelia. There were some issues there, but I'm hoping they have been resolved. Wait just a bit before returning if you can, okay? Talk to her. She helped fight Adrien, and she now runs the city. She will make sure you find housing and work."

Millie scurried away just as Beth entered, holding a cup of her own tea, and a woven bag brimming with wool and needles.

"Oh, no, did Millie upset you?" Beth asked, eyes wide.

Julianne smiled. "Quite the opposite. I'm so sorry if I've upset things here, but I gave her a letter of recommendation." Julianne watched Beth as she explained. "She said she wanted to go back to Arcadia."

"Oh, how wonderful!" Beth gushed, and Julianne relaxed. "We do take in as many as we can, but our own income is quite pitiful. We simply can't afford to give the poor souls what they need to make a fresh start."

"Millie said Nathan saved her from a cruel master," Julianne queried. "What kind of estate are you running here?"

Beth gave a conspiratorial smile. "It's a railroad," she whispered.

Julianne frowned, confused. "A what?"

"A railroad, a secret one. Nathan read it in a book, once—we save the slaves and the ones who are trapped under cruel masters. We train them up, give them a home and good food, and then they leave when they're ready."

Beth pulled out a thin, hooked needle and a bit of thread

attached to a square of knitted cloth. She thrust the needle through, looped the thread around and pulled it back out.

"You're doing a wonderful thing," Julianne said quietly. "I think Nathan was wrong when he said you wouldn't live up to your namesakes. Seems like you already have."

Beth continued working as a tiny smile tugged at one side of her mouth. "I know. Silly old man can't see it, but I know."

CHAPTER SIXTEEN

"We had no choice!" Patrick, one of the captured bandits, spat on the ground beside him, his saliva tinged pink with blood.

His white makeup had smudged onto his shirt, leaving patches of flushed pink skin peeking through the disguise. He sniffed, then rolled his shoulder, pulling on the bindings around his wrists again.

"There's always a choice, ye selfish bastard." Garrett resisted the urge to kick the fallen man in the face, opting instead to aim at a clump of dirt, showering it over Patrick.

"We were living on our own just fine!" Patrick growled. "Sure, we picked a few travelers pockets and raided the odd campsite, but we never killed anyone. You want a fight? Go pick one with the remnant that raided our settlement."

"Remnant?" Garrett barked a caustic laugh. "Ye wouldn't know a remnant if it bit ye on the ass."

Patrick growled and lunged against his restraints. "I've seen them! And I've fought them, too! Lost half our band to the crazed scum."

"The way ye fight, I'm surprised ye didn't lose more," Bette said easily. She swaggered over. "And yer costumes? I've seen wee children dress more convincingly at the festivals."

It was Patrick's turn to laugh. "Didn't stop anyone we approached from pissing their pants and running for the hills. Even seasoned fighters!" His eyes narrowed. "You might say, we saved lives with these costumes. They ran, we ate. I'm not apologizing for that."

This time Garrett did kick him, a firm, booted toe in the ribs. Not hard enough to break anything, but Patrick buckled over, gasping for breath anyway.

"That's enough, Garrett," Bette warned. "Ye know the lord wouldn't approve of ye roughing up the prisoners. At least, not until we get 'em back ta Tahn."

Patrick paled. "You're taking us captive?"

Bette laughed. "What did ye think? That we'd set ye on yer merry way, off ta loot and plunder our trading routes?"

Patrick slumped back, grumbling something under his breath.

"Well, I did suggest we leave ye behind," Garrett said. Patrick looked up, warily. "Aye, I did! Dead men can't cause no trouble on the roads, and it'd be a might bit easier than luggin' yer heavy asses back with us."

Patrick closed his eyes and muttered a prayer as Bette turned her back. "I'll go see if old George is done with our Francis yet."

She stalked over to the carriage and poked her head in, just as Francis stepped out the other side onto wobbly legs.

"Och, what did ye say to the lad?" she asked George.

"Oh, I just impressed on him the importance of what I have bestowed," George said. "But you should know—he's your lord, now. He's sworn fealty to me, but you will lead beneath him. And, perhaps call him something other than 'lad', eh?" He raised a knowing eyebrow, and Bette blushed.

"Apologies, my lord. I'll see young—er, Lord Francis is shown all the respect he deserves. Even if I have to break a few knees ta do it," she added, grinning.

"Now, I don't think that's necessary," George said, though he smiled, too. "The boy has a knack for negotiation, I see—he insisted that remuneration for the Captain and First Lieutenant of Tahn are both paid out of Muir's coffers, and at a higher rate than you're getting."

"That's not necessary, my lord," Bette protested.

"It is if I want him to lead his people." George darted a glance out his window. "And to be fair, I'd be dead if you hadn't been here. It might be prudent to—"

He was interrupted by the sound of a horn, high and clear in the crisp afternoon air.

"Attack! Remnant are attacking!" Came the first cry, and right on its heels, "Bandits! More bandits!"

"Ach, ye sly bastard," Bette hissed. "Francis! Back in the carriage, stay with George."

She raced over to Garrett, and this time, it was her boot that met Patrick's ribs. "Ye sneaky shit, who are they?"

Patrick's eyes were wide, his face white. "Not mine," he gasped. "Please—please, you can't fight them! They're insane!"

"Bullshit," Garrett leaned down into Patrick's face. "They're yer friends, back to save yer ass!"

Patrick shook his head, a swift, jerking motion. "No. You caught all of us. They're..." he swallowed. "They're either impersonators, or..."

Screams from the back of the party sent Garrett and Bette running. They leapt over bags and carts strewn in their way, bolting for the sound of terror. When they found it, they screeched to a halt.

A ragged figure stabbed down with a cackle and lifted his eyes to Bette.

Red eyes.

The band of seven remnant—*real* remnant—had taken out four soldiers already. One of the beasts was down, bucking in agony and clutching his face.

"Oh, shit," Garrett whispered.

"Aye," Bette agreed. "Shit."

As one, they launched into a run. Garrett wielded an axe, short-handled and perfectly balanced, sharp blade glittering in the afternoon sun. Bette swung her sword in lazy loops as she picked up speed.

They crashed into the fray, shouldering George's troops aside as they pushed through to the enemy.

Garrett's axe bit into a dirt-crusted thigh. Bette's sword slammed into a soft, filth-streaked belly.

"For George!" They hollered as the fighting crashed in around them.

Weapons flew, and blood splashed, then gushed. Bette was pummeled by three remnant, all weighing down on top of her. She stumbled and fell, squashed flat by the weight.

With a mighty heave, she lifted her body, pushing up to rest on her hands and knees. Then, with a roar, she shoved herself back. The remnant tumbled off, one taking a hunk of her hair with it.

Pain stung her scalp and stoked her fury. She whirled, eyes landing on the angry beast still holding a long ribbon of hair, bloody patch of scalp attached. It looked at her and grinned.

"We kill your pack leader, ugly bitch, and make you watch," it cackled. *"DIE!"*

"Ye whimpering, pig-fuckin', slug-eatin', rat testicle! I *am* the fucking pack leader!" She screamed, before running at him, sword tucked neatly at her side.

She thrust it forward at the last minute, stabbing the remnant at the base of the throat. It jerked, spasmed, and died in a matter of moments.

Bette spun to face another remnant, poised to stab a rusted spear through a man on the ground. She saw who it was and groaned.

"And what the fuck're ye doin'—" she grunted at the remnant, blade cutting into his side with a solid whump, "—tryin' ta hurt me prisoner?"

She pulled it free and fended off its return attack with a well-placed boot that sent the remnant tumbling onto its back. Bette jumped, landing one foot on its windpipe, the other on its chest as she parried a thrust from another attacker.

She fought, her balance precarious on the fleshy, struggling platform. The remnant stabbed at her and hit, stinging heat spreading through her shoulder.

She whipped her sword around and sliced off her target's head, then tripped, landing face down in the dirt. Rough hands yanked her back up. She whirled to come face to face with Patrick. A frantic look around showed no further fighting, and she sucked in a steadying breath.

"Thank you," he said.

"Who the fuck let ye out?" she snapped.

He shrugged. "One of the soldiers. A remnant slipped by you into the camp, I told him I could kill it."

Bette's heart jumped. "Did ye?"

He nodded briskly. "Don't worry, it wasn't an act of altruism. He took one look at me and decided I was the one he meant to kill."

She laughed. "That bloody costume yer wearin' pissed him off."

Bette dashed back into the camp. "Francis?" she yelled. "George?"

She reached the carriage, which now had a huge indent on one side and chunks taken from the carved wood. She yanked the door open and a blade sprang out, unsteady, but pointed at her face.

She drew back, hands raised, while she waited for Francis to slowly drop the weapon.

"Oh, Bitch! Sorry, Bette," he stammered.

"Och, don't be apologizin', lad—lord." She grinned. "Ye were ready for trouble, that's what I like to see!"

Francis gave a nervous laugh, then looked up, his face darkening. "Bette! Your shoulder!"

She brushed off his concern. "Just a flesh wound," she said. "And a lot of remnant blood. Here, let me help ye down."

Francis waited for Bette to reach out, but she stood, a blank look on her face. "Oh, shit. I can't move me arm. Maybe it's a wee bit worse than I…"

Color draining from her face, Bette toppled over before she could finish. Francis jumped down, catching her roughly before she landed on the dirt-packed road.

"Oh, hell," Francis muttered. Then, with all the might he could muster, screamed for help. "*GARRETT!*"

CHAPTER SEVENTEEN

Bastian slung his pack over his shoulder and stepped outside, then jumped when Tansy appeared beside him.

"Going somewhere, Bastian?" she asked casually.

Bastian looked over at his companion. She wore her hair tied back in a braid, and a heavy leather corset with matching pants. Her belt held a sword, two throwing knives and a water skein.

"I was going to come and see you," he said defensively.

"Then it's a good thing I was ready," she said. "Now you don't have to come and find me!"

He laughed as they headed for the gates. Carey waved at them as they passed. "Be careful out there!" he called.

"Will do!" Bastian replied heartily. "How is Bette? I heard she came back injured last night."

Carey nodded. "She'll live, though Garrett may not if he doesn't leave her alone. Damn bandits!"

Bastian waved goodbye and stepped outside the boundary of the small town he had grown to love.

"Are you sure this is a good idea, Bastian?" Tansy asked. "Bandits roaming the roads, *ghosts* in the forest." She waggled her fingers spookily and made a 'woo' sound.

"You really think Bette and Garrett left any bandits alive?" Bastian chuckled. "If anyone in Tahn hurt Bette like that, Garrett would raze the whole place to the ground. Not even the mice would make it out alive."

"They're such a sweet couple," Tansy said, clasping her hands to her chest.

Bastian snorted. "They're as sweet as two angry bulls," he said. "I don't know how they haven't killed each other already."

Tansy rolled her eyes. "You men—you just have no idea."

"Hey, I know what I want in a woman," Bastian protested.

"Oh?" Tansy asked, a dangerous glint in her eyes. "What's that?"

Bastian grinned. "One who knows that I'm just a stupid man with lots to learn."

Tansy slapped him. "You're an idiot, Bastian."

"Isn't that what I said?"

They fell silent for a short while as they walked. The effort made Bastian warm under his robes, and his pack weighed heavy on his shoulder. He hoisted it up, adjusting the strap.

"What's in there?" Tansy asked. "I hope it's lunch."

"I brought my papers," he said. "I need to make measurements, and lists for Francis."

"You mean *Lord* Francis," Tansy reminded him. "What's it like to have the ear of the local nobility?"

Bastian laughed. "It's just Francis. He's not the sort to get all high and mighty because he has a title."

"How does one become a lord, anyway?" Tansy asked. "I mean, I know Lord George gave the title to Francis, and he inherited his from his father… but how'd he get the title?"

Bastian shrugged. "When the world started to rebuild, he just took it," Bastian said. "George followed his father's footsteps. Back home, the nobility mostly bought their titles, or took them once they'd built up their fortunes or estates. Well, before the chancellor started making that harder, anyway."

"So, I could call myself Lady Tansy and no one could argue with me?"

"Well, they could argue, but it's not like there's a law against it." Bastian frowned, thinking. "No one would take you seriously, though, unless you could show you had a fortune to back you, or land or power."

Tansy fell silent, then laughed. "So, *you* can call yourself a lord! You'll have the school, that's a kind of power, and—"

"No," Bastian said flatly. "I've seen what happens when a center of education is tainted by power. No one will ever run my school for profit, *or* for power."

Tansy slid a glance his way. "You know, there are some that would say that's an honorable stance, Bastian."

"Are you one of them?" he asked.

Tansy shrugged. "I don't know much about honor. But you're a good man, Bastian. And that's hard to find."

Bastian's cheeks flushed with heat. *Must be the exertion*, he assured himself. That's all it is. He ignored the butterflies in his stomach, and the thrill of knowing Tansy thought he was a 'good man'.

They reached the Iron Tree and stopped for a moment in the shade of the forest, both shivering as the breeze cooled their sweat-dampened skin. Just in the day since they had last visited, more patches of dappled sunlight peeked through the gaps left by fallen leaves.

"Winter won't be far away," Tansy said quietly. "It will look a whole lot different here then."

Bastian suppressed another shiver at the thought of naked trees reaching bare branches into the sky, unsure why the image disturbed him.

"Why, Bastian," Tansy said in surprise. "You're not getting creeped out, are you?" She laughed.

"What? Me?" he blustered. "No way. There's nothing out here to be scared of."

He took off down the trail leading to the ruins, leaving her to catch up.

When they reached the empty space in the forest, Tansy snorted. "Yeah," she said. "Nothing at all to be afraid of… except for whatever left *that*."

She pointed at something on the ground, and when Bastian came over to get a closer look, his heart jumped into his mouth. The little pile of bones had been stripped clean and piled up too neatly to be left by a wild animal.

"Just a passing traveler," he said, voice wavering. "Like us."

"Or…" Tansy whispered, leaning close to his ear. "Bandits!" she yelled and then laughed when he jumped away like he had been stabbed.

"Bastard's oath, Tansy!" Bastian yelped. "If my nerves weren't shot before, they are now!"

"So, you *are* scared of the forest!" She clapped her hands happily, then jumped, twirling, and landed in an exaggerated fight pose. "Never fear, Bastian, my dear! Your fearless protector will keep you safe!"

"You look more likely to fall on your face, if you plan to fight like that," Bastian pointed out.

Tansy pouted. "Fine. You have your fun, but don't come crying to me when the ghost of the witchtree comes to eat your face off."

"If anyone's going to eat my face, it'll be—" Bastian stopped, realizing that what he just said might be construed very differently to what he had meant.

"Bastian!" Tansy gasped, clapping a hand over her mouth. "I've never been so shocked in all my life!"

"I didn't mean that!" he protested. "I swear, I wouldn't—"

Tansy laughed again, and Bastian growled. "You were making fun of me again?" He asked. "This is why I don't spend time with people. They're all too damn clever, and I just end up looking like a fool."

Tansy softened and wrapped an arm around him. "I'm sorry, book-boy. You're just easy to tease, that's all, and now that the cranky old geezer Artemis is gone, everyone is looking for a new target. But I promise I'll lay off, ok?"

Bastian shrugged her arm off. "I'll believe it when I see it," he said. Then, his unease forgotten, he dumped his pack on the ground and pulled out a sheaf of parchment. "Here, can you hold this while I step out the measurements?"

Tansy took the stack of clean, cream-colored parchment, balancing it so the pen didn't roll off the top. "Sure. I'm here to help, after all."

Bastian didn't answer, instead weighing the end of a string down with a stone and trailing it along the edge of a wall. At the other end, he gathered the string back up, counting the little tied-off markers as he went.

Tansy held out the pieces of parchment and he scratched a rough box on the top one, then marked the length on one side. He measured the next length, nervously glancing through the gap he had climbed through the day before.

He measured the remains of the crumbling walls, then, with a hesitant look beyond, asked Tansy if she could help him find the water source he had heard.

"If it's clean and deep, it will make everything easier," he explained.

Tansy agreed happily, but smirked as he timidly peeked through the gap in the wall.

"It's ok," she reassured him. "I won't let anything eat you. Or your face." She snickered, bit her lip, and then burst out, "Unless you ask."

Bastian groaned and shook his head. He cupped one ear and swung around slowly, then pointed. "Can you hear that?"

"What, ghosts?" she asked before giggling again.

Bastian rolled his eyes and groaned again. Tansy smoothed her face and furrowed her brow, cocking one head to listen.

"A stream!" she exclaimed, taking the lead and climbing over a fallen tree, towards the sound of flowing water.

They pushed through overgrown bushes and lanky branches until they found the source of the noise. A brook, flowing down over a small, rocky fall, pooled in a deep pond. A frog croaked loudly and jumped into the water, flitting away on strong legs as a bird cawed and took flight at the intrusion.

"Oh," Bastian said. "This is perfect!"

"It's a bit dirty," Tansy pointed out with a frown.

In the swirling eddy where the water flowed into the main reservoir, a scrap of cloth swirled and dipped with other debris. Bastian picked up a fallen branch and leaned over to nudge the collection.

A rotted apple with a bite taken out; a length of frayed rope; a cracked wooden bowl. A chill rippled down Bastian's spine as he remembered the remnant campsites he had passed in the Madlands.

"That could be from anywhere," he said to Tansy. "It's just rubbish, like you'd find in town. Maybe it's drifted all the way from Muir."

Tansy looked up at the sun, then turned slowly. "I don't think so," she said. "Unless that watercourse crawls around the valley between here and there. There are other cities beyond that, sure, but they're ages away."

"So… campers. Travelers, bandits. They all leave rubbish behind, right?" Bastian looked at her, pleading.

She shrugged. "I guess so. I mean, what else can it be? Ghosts don't use bowls, or ropes."

Bastian squashed down the thought of remnant and pulled back. "Anyway," he said. "I've got everything I need. Let's go."

"Already?" Tansy asked. "Can't we stop for lunch first?"

Bastian gave a nervous laugh. "Always thinking about your stomach," he said. "I guess we have time."

When they got back to the ruins, he let Tansy climb through the fallen bit of wall first, as he cast one last worried look out over to the forest. The trees, too dense to offer a view of the water, shifted in the breeze and shades of moss and lichen almost hid the green and white painted face that stared back at him.

"Tansy?" he said, then cleared his throat and tried again. "Tansy!"

"What, you need me to lift you over?" she teased, sticking her head out. When she saw Bastian's wide eyes and frozen look of terror, she turned her eyes to the forest. "What, did you see a ghost?" she asked.

Bastian blinked. The face was gone. "There was… a face. Tansy, I saw someone! A face looking back at me!"

Tansy scanned the trees again. "Nope. Not seeing it. Or do you mean that knotted bit of bark? It *kind* of looks like a face."

He shook his head and pointed to the gap between some branches where it had peered out at him. "It was over there!"

"You want me to go look?" she asked, sticking her leg through the wall.

"No!" he yelped, shoving her foot back through the gap. "We have to go. Now!"

He scrambled through and grabbed his bag, hurriedly shoving papers into it before swinging it over his back. He drew a long knife from one of the pockets.

"Damn Artemis for stealing that amphorald," he muttered. He debated, just for a moment, reaching out to Julianne. *She can't help, she's too far way*, he realized.

Grabbing Tansy's hand, he ran for the trail. As his feet slapped on the final stone, something moved ahead.

Bastian stumbled, trying to stop. Tansy screamed. A snarling figure blocked the path, armed with a long spear. Lesions on his face peeked through the layer of mossy stains and his clothes, rotted and falling apart, barely covered him.

"Remnant," Bastian gasped.

"This Chet's land!" the remnant growled. "You will be sacrificed to Chet!"

CHAPTER EIGHTEEN

Julianne carefully folded her clothes, freshly washed by Beth's maids and already dry from a few hours by the fireplace. A hard stone in her bag nudged at her hand and she drew it out again.

"I thought I got rid of this," she mused.

She debated offering it to Beth as a parting gift, but decided instead to leave it as a surprise. Julianne placed it gently on the mantle in her room, and packed the rest of her things away.

Her missing papers hadn't appeared, and the weight of that settled on her like lead. Though the letters of introduction could be replaced, Selah's note was personal, and he was gone now.

Throwing off her sadness, Julianne vowed to move forwards. She needed to focus on getting back to the Heights—and finding Donna.

"I get the feeling I won't have to look hard," she muttered, sure that Donna would seek her out.

"Are you ready?" Marcus stuck his head in the door, hair flopping over his face. "Beth wants us to have breakfast with them before we leave."

"Yes," she said. "But maybe we should have asked if any of Beth's maids can cut hair."

Marcus frowned. "Why? Your hair looks fine."

Julianne tousled his fringe as she passed him. "Mine is. Yours? Not so much."

"Hey! I like my hair like this!" Marcus called as he hurried down the hallway after her.

They dined in the kitchen, Julianne, Marcus, and Artemis crowded at a long table amongst Beth, Nathan, and six of their staff. The conversation was loud and happy, as butter and bread were passed from one end to the other, and big glops of porridge were dropped into bowls from three seats down.

"Reminds me of Annie's," Julianne whispered to Marcus wistfully. "And home."

"Well, I can't speak for home," Marcus pointed out. "But yeah, Annie's was like this."

Julianne enjoyed the babble quietly, eating the last of her meal slowly to draw it out as long as she could. Finally, her bowl scraped clean and the conversation waning, she stood.

"Beth, Nathan, I can't thank you enough for the hospitality you've offered." She gathered her plate to take it to the basin.

"Oh, don't you go doing that, ma'am!" Millie jumped up and started clearing the table. "We've all been so glad to have you here."

Julianne clasped Millie's arm, then pulled her into a light hug. "I meant what I said. If any of you come to Arcadia, just mention my name. I'll make sure you get work somewhere safe."

Millie dabbed at her eyes and ducked her head. "Thank you, ma'am. I'm not ready to go just yet—it's like leaving family behind here. But when I do, I'll make sure to send word, so you'll know how I get on."

"I might even visit you one day," Julianne said, beaming. She hoped she would be able to find the time, but a shadow passed over her heart as she thought on what she would have to do first.

Bloody Rogan, she thought. *Still haunting me, even after I put you in the grave.*

Determined not to let it spoil the morning, Julianne stood tall and said goodbye to everyone, shaking hands and accepting more than one kiss on the cheek.

"Marcus, could you grab my bags?" she whispered to one side. "I've left them upstairs."

He nodded and darted away, returning a minute later with her two satchels. "I'll go ready our horses," he said.

"Wonderful. Artemis, are you—" Julianne realized he was gone. "Oh, that man. If he's off wandering the fields again, I'll leave him behind!"

"Oh, he'll be saying his farewell to our Bethany," Nathan said. "She'll make sure he doesn't get lost on his way out, much as she'd like to keep him here."

Nathan was right. By the time the horses were saddled and packed and Julianne had made her way outside, Artemis was by the door, hand in hand with a glittery-eyed Beth.

"Now," she said in a choked voice. "You make sure it's not so long between visits this time, you hear?" She patted his chest firmly, then rested her hand on his shirt.

"Well… it'll be some time before I can return, but if I'm welcome, I might just make it my last stop," Artemis said.

Beth's face lit up in a bright smile. "Then I'll wait for you just as I did before." She gave him one last pat, then stepped back, her hands dropping away as if they no longer had a purpose.

"Strike me down with a feather," Marcus muttered. "This trip has been one surprise after another. You think he means it?"

Julianne nodded. "Every word. I'd best get my information out of him as fast as I can when we get back to the Temple, or he might just leave before we're done."

"Speaking of the Temple," Marcus said. "We might just make it back tonight, if we leave now and ride hard."

Julianne gnawed at her lip, then jerked her head in a nod. "Let's. I don't want to wait longer than we need."

They walked the horses down the shaded path back to the

road, and kicked the horses into a run once they were there, much to Artemis's distress.

They rode through the day, only stopping for a brief time to rest and water the horses when their shadows shrank to nothing and the sun lightly bled the ground. Even the brief stop was enough to make Julianne shiver when she climbed back up on Cloud's back.

"The weather turned quickly," she remarked to Marcus as they walked along the empty road.

"You're just normally coddled up in a big stone castle when winter hits," he pointed out. "For us less fortunate folk, we live through this every year."

"Less fortunate?" Julianne asked, an eyebrow shooting up. "Less fortunate as in, you didn't have freshly pressed clothes delivered every morning, or hot meals three times a day or a warm, dry place to sleep?"

Marcus stretched, cracking his spine. "You always take everything so literally."

"You're walking into an ambush," Julianne said pleasantly.

"Like I couldn't see that coming. I adore you, Jules, but leading me into these loaded discussions always leaves me feeling like I've put a foot wrong."

Julianne frowned, then laughed. "No, Marcus. A *literal* ambush. There are four men waiting for us to pass under them. They plan to scare the horses, so we're thrown off, then rob us blind."

"Oh. Well at least this trip won't all be boring." Marcus slowed, waiting for her to give instructions.

Julianne sat still in her saddle as Cloud Dancer slowly ambled on towards the waiting men. Her eyes shone white, and her posture was relaxed.

"Marcus," she said in a low voice. "This isn't right."

"Well… yeah, we're about to be hit by bandits. There's nothing *right* about that!" He edged his horse closer to hers, concerned at her hesitance.

"That's just it. I have control of one of the men, and he's *not* a bandit. They're traders." Julianne's brow furrowed in concentration.

"Why are they jumping us, then?" Marcus asked.

Julianne shrugged. "He doesn't know. Marcus, this feels a lot like the compulsion that hit two rearick on our way out of the Temple." She gave him a quick explanation and he nodded. "Artemis?" she asked. "What do you think?"

Artemis snorted. "I couldn't say. My ass is too sore from all that bouncing around."

Marcus groaned. "So, you think Donna passed through?" he asked Julianne.

Julianne nodded. "But… this compulsion is buried deep. I don't know if I can undo it soon enough to stop them. And I don't want to hurt them for something they can't help doing."

"What if we knock them over the head?" Marcus shrugged. "That seems to solve most problems."

Julianne clicked her tongue. "Marcus! I'm not beating innocent men over the head! Especially if I can't be sure it will work. They might wake up and hurt themselves, like some of Rogan's victims did."

"Or, track us down and murder us while we sleep." Marcus grinned to take the edge off his words. "Look, we'll take them down gently, then tie them up. You can play in their heads while I raid the rations. I'm absolutely starving."

"You ate three plates at breakfast!" she reminded him dryly. "And if this holds us up too long, we won't make it back to the Temple in time to eat."

"Then I'll just have to make sure I save you some." Marcus slid off his horse and wrapped the reins around his hand, making sure the animal had plenty of slack. Marcus didn't want to lose his fingers if the horse took fright and reared up.

Julianne joined him on the ground, holding Cloud's reins loosely. She had worked with the horse long enough now that she was sure Cloud would return even if something scared the usually stalwart mare away.

Marcus watched Julianne instead of the trees. Her connection with the trader would give her more notice of an attack than any sign he saw.

When she faltered just slightly, placing a foot down and hesitating for the barest of moments, Marcus drew his sword with a zing. He spun around as the leaves above rustled and three men jumped from the branches.

The thud of feet behind him, followed by the crack of Julianne's wooden staff on hard bone made him smile. He didn't turn to check on her, confident her skills matched his own.

Marcus slammed the flat edge of his blade against the round stomach of the nearest man. He bent over in pain, and Marcus turned to the next. He led with his blade, swinging it towards the terrified trader's neck.

At the last minute, he turned it away and while his opponent tried to duck the feinted swing, Marcus shoved a boot into his chest. The man gasped and stumbled back.

"Catch!" Marcus looked up at Julianne's cry just in time to snatch a length of rope she had thrown at him.

It uncoiled, one end slithering to the ground, and the trader squealed as it touched his leg.

"It's just rope," Marcus said, and the man stopped trying to squirm away, but lay muttering quietly to himself.

Marcus bent closer to hear what he was saying.

"Must… must stop her. Have to stop her."

"Stop who?" Marcus asked.

The trader stilled, eyes stretched into wide circles as they rolled back to look in Julianne's direction. "*Her.*"

CHAPTER NINETEEN

Bette groaned and cracked open an eyelid. "Who put that bloody light on?" she muttered. "Turn it off."

She reached down to pull her blanket over her head to block out the offensive glow, but a stab of pain shot her eyes open. "Bloody hell!"

"Ah, yer awake!" Garrett's face swam in front of hers as the room blurred. "Settle yer wee self, lassie. Still short a few drops of blood, ye are." He pressed a gentle hand against her good shoulder, and she collapsed back into bed.

Bette panted with the pain, trying to think through her sudden panic. "The remnant. George!"

"Aye, old George is tucked up back in his own bed," Garrett reassured her. "Ye didn't keel over until the remnant were all dead."

"What about that bastard bandit?" she asked.

Garrett shrugged. "He's back under guard at Muir with the rest of his ugly friends." He held out a wooden cup. "Here, wet yer lips."

Bette took a big gulp. Acrid tang filled her mouth, and she

spat it back out, showering Garrett with brown liquid. "Fuck! Yer tryin' to poison me, ye prick?"

Garrett dabbed a sleeve to his face, then pulled back, sniffed it with a disgusted look. "Stinks, doesn't it? Drink it anyway, ye pansy. It'll help yer blood rebuild and take the edge off the pain."

"I don't—" Bette began.

"Ye don't need it?" Garrett asked. "Aye, that suits me. The longer you're in bed, the longer I get to run the guard!" He grinned gleefully.

Bette stared at him for a moment, then her eyes dropped to the cup. Screwing up her face, she downed the dark sludge in one gulp.

"I'll be back on me feet by tomorrow," she snapped. "Go get me more of… more…" The room twirled around, and she watched as tiny stars dipped and swam through the air. Warmth suffused her limbs as her muscles weakened.

"Yerr balfurd." The mangled slur sounded nothing like what she had intended to say. She tried again, but when her mouth opened, a giant yawn filled her lungs as her body slumped back into the pillow.

"Aye," said one of Garrett's heads. The other one smiled. "Ye get some rest and ye'll be right as rain in no time."

I'll chop off both yer heads tomorrow, Bette thought as darkness surrounded her and she slipped back into sleep.

Garrett patted Bette's hair. When her eyes drifted shut, his smile drifted into a scowl. "She'll have my *fuckin'* ass fer that later," he grumbled. "Bitch help me."

He stalked out of the room and into the kitchen, where Mary stood by the stove. "Did she drink it?" she asked.

Garrett nodded. "Sleeping like a wee babe. Do ye think she might forget that I tricked her into it?"

Mary chuckled. "With luck, yes. But don't let her near any sharp weapons when she first wakes." She patted a hand on a cloth-wrapped pot. "There's some broth in here. Give that to her before anything solid. It'll be nice and gentle on her stomach. It should keep warm for some time."

Garrett sucked in a deep breath and sighed contentedly. "Mary, if I ever get stabbed in the arm, will ye make me some of that?"

Mary shook her head and headed for the door. "There's enough for two, don't worry. No need to create an emergency just for some old soup."

Garrett grinned and leaned over to give her a quick hug as she passed. "Thank ye, lass. I'll make sure Bette knows ye were lookin' after her."

"Me and half the town," Mary said as she pulled the door open. A pile of flowers and candles tumbled inside.

Garrett gaped, then scrubbed his suddenly stinging eyes. "Aye," he said. "I'll let her know."

He saw Mary out, hugging her again before she took off down the street. Spotting Danil headed out of town, Garrett called him over.

"Mystic! Get yer blind arse over here," Garrett yelled.

Danil looked up and grinned. He lifted his thin cane from the road and tucked it under his arm as he headed over.

"Do ye know who has been doing all this?" Garrett asked as he gathered up the gifts left at his doorstep.

"It would be easier to tell you who *hasn't*," Danil said. "That would be… well, no one."

"What?" Garrett said, dumping the wilting flowers on the table. "We only came in last night. Who the bloody hell organized it?"

"You flew through those gates screaming for a medic," Danil reminded him. "We thought Bette was dead, or close to it. Half the town heard the ruckus!"

Garrett turned away, stomping over to a tiny cupboard and

pulling out some cups. He filled them with water from the tiny kitchen pump, then lined them up on the table. "I wasn't that loud," he grumbled as he fed bunches of wildflowers into the cups. "And if ye'd seen the blood, ye'd have been worried, too!"

Dani gave a soft chuckle and straightened a crooked stalk of lavender. "We were, rearick. We were. The whole town cares for Bette—and for you."

"Me? Why the *bloody* hell would they do a silly thing like that?" Garrett snapped.

"Because you saved them from the Dawn. I know, Julianne did the hardest part, but you and Bette didn't just fight alongside her. You taught them to fight for themselves. You gave them a kind of freedom you can't just hand over. You let them earn it." Danil tapped the table restlessly.

"Aye." Garrett sat down with a thump. "And I won't deny the sight of all that blood..." he shuddered.

Danil reached out and squeezed Garrett's arm. "We know how much you care for her. You're allowed to be concerned."

"Aye. I'm glad ta have those around that care," Garrett admitted. "It's not like the Heights, that's fer damn sure!"

Danil sighed and tapped the table again. "I'm leaving," he said.

"What, yer headed to the hall?" Garrett asked.

Danil's face dropped. "No, Garrett. I'm leaving Tahn."

"What?" Garrett shot up in his chair. "Ye can't go! Not yet, not while Bette's—"

"Not now," Danil reassured him. "Not for a while, actually. But once Bastian's school is underway, and once I know Julianne is back at the Temple safe and sound... well, Polly and I want to go somewhere."

"Where?" Garrett screwed up his face, confused. "Tahn has food and beer. The whiskey's not much, but it'll do. What else could ye want?"

Danil stared at the table, a small smile on his lips. "Adventure.

Garrett, I barely left the Temple when I lived there. Sure, a few trips to Arcadia if I couldn't avoid them. But even my pilgrimage didn't take me as far as we've travelled together."

"Ye got the bug," Garrett said. "Aye, it happens to us mountain folk, too. Most of us like to stick close to home, but some? Oh, those ones will walk ta the ends o' the stars and beyond."

Danil looked up at that. "Do you think they *have* an end?"

"What?" Garrett cocked his head.

"The stars. Do you think they have an end? All the old legends say that's where Queen Bethany Anne went. I wonder how far she got?"

Garrett snorted. "What, ye plannin' ta go look for 'er? Bah. Half the stories are just that—stories."

"You'd be surprised," Danil said quietly, thinking back on the reams of paper, books, and pictures kept back at the Temple. "But either way, we're going to go. I just need to break it to Bastian."

Garrett winced. "I don't envy ye that job. But if yer off ta do it now, tell the lad not ta leave Tahn for a bit, eh? With those monsters runnin' about the woods…"

"What?" Danil said, jolting up in his seat. "I thought you killed all the bandits."

"Bandits?" Garrett barked a laugh. "I guess ye were all too busy worrying about Bette ta pay attention ta the real worry. They were *remnant*, lad! Remnant, runnin' about like nobody's business. We killed the ones we saw, but I don't want people wanderin' around until we have a nose around, like."

Danil stood quickly, knocking over his chair. He leaned over the table, eyes pleading. "No, Garrett. You don't understand— Bastian has already gone!"

"What?" Garrett screeched, jumping up and racing for the door. He doubled back to grab a sword off the floor by the fire where he had discarded it the night before, too exhausted to do more than clean it.

Garrett paused, eyes darting to the closed bedroom door.

"I'll stay," Danil said. "I'll look after her, Garrett, just… please. Don't let Bastian get hurt?"

Garrett nodded in thanks and sprinted out the door, hollering for Sharne and Carey.

CHAPTER TWENTY

The remnant jumped, thrusting the spear forwards at Bastian. Tansy shoved him out of the way, pirouetting so that it missed her as well. She flung a foot around and connected with the remnant's leg, making him stumble.

He recovered quickly, stabbing at her three times, his movement quick but fluid. Tansy scrambled back and yanked her knives out, gripping one in each hand.

Bastian ran at the beast, knife pointed forwards. The remnant turned and slammed him in the chest with the spear butt, sending Bastian sprawling on the ground, legs in the air.

The remnant took a step, then staggered as Tansy's right hit him in the back. Its throat blossomed, then sprayed blood as her knife flashed in a stray beam of sunlight.

Tansy shoved the writhing body away and stood, hands on her knees, trembling. Bastian scrambled to his feet.

"Are you ok?" he asked, breath short and gasping.

She nodded, then straightened. "Yes, I'm—" she stopped, and her lip trembled for a moment. Then, sucking in a hard breath, she spoke quickly. "Fine. I'm fine, but we should go."

Bastian nodded. He grabbed his dropped pack and took her

arm, walking quickly through the dense foliage. The forest crackled and shifted, each tiny noise sending a spike of fear racing through Tansy's heart.

Gripping her knives—she had dropped the sword and forgotten to go back for it before they left—Tansy forced her mind to the worn trail ahead. Yet, the twisted face of the remnant kept rocking its way into her thoughts.

She shuddered. "Are they all like that?" she asked quietly.

Bastian nodded. "More or less. But they normally travel in packs, so—"

A loud crack behind them startled Tansy, and she jumped, whirling. Two hunched figures, as twisted and ugly as the first, blocked the path behind them.

"Run!" she screamed and pushed Bastian forwards.

She ran, years of practice at running and jumping lending her feet speed and balance. The remnant were fast, too, though. The slap of footsteps inched closer, and their mangled growls were too close.

Bastian tripped. He fell, his momentum skidding him along the dirt until he came to a painful stop.

A shriek of glee behind them made Tansy's breath catch. She dove off the path, into the trees as the remnant pounced on Bastian.

She spotted a young, thin sapling stretching high into the shadowed canopy. Beside it, a sturdier tree covered in knots and stubby branches gave her an idea.

Tansy scaled the thicker tree, lifting herself up like a cat skittering up a wall. She jumped onto a branch and threw herself through the air, landing on a thicker branch, as balanced as she would be during a well-rehearsed performance.

A quick look down at the ground below made her grin. "This is no tent," she muttered as quick steps brought the sapling into view.

Tansy took a second to check her balance, standing with two

feet securely on the wider branch as she stared at the swaying tip of the smaller tree.

"One… two… listen to the crowd roar." Narrowing her focus, she blew out a sharp breath.

She hurled herself forwards, grabbing the sapling with one hand. It stretched and bent, the pliant trunk building tension as it lowered her to the ground… right before a remnant.

She swung, wrapping her legs around the tree and freeing her hands. When she grabbed the startled remnant, yanking his flimsy shirt over a nub protruding from the trunk, she wondered if she had any chance of her plan working.

She dropped down and kicked the remnant, shoving him further onto the tree as the spring-loaded trunk was relieved of her weight. It shot up into the air, taking the screaming remnant with it.

Tansy punched the air, then fell forwards as something hit her from behind.

"Oh, you can't let a girl celebrate?" she asked, falling into a roll and coming back up on her feet. She grinned, tipping her head to one side as the remnant charged her.

"Hot head," she teased, stepping to one side at the last minute.

The remnant skidded to a halt and turned, roaring in wordless fury. It dropped into a low stance, breathing hard. "Chet take city!" he growled. "Not yours. *DIE!*"

His scream sent birds shooting into the air as he jumped.

Tansy darted to the side, but this time, he was ready. A hand darted out and grabbed her shirt, pulling her to the ground. The remnant rolled on top of her.

Tansy kicked, swinging her weight from her legs to overturn him. She overcommitted, though, and the roll that was meant to land her in the dominant position took her right back to where she had started.

A hand clamped down on her throat.

"Monster took our home," the remnant hissed. His breath

smelled of death and rotting rust. "Now, we take yours. *We* monster now."

Tansy choked, hands scrabbling at his wrists. She dug her nails in, tearing his flesh, but he didn't budge.

Darkness swam at the edges of her vision. Her eyes drifted shut as a thud vibrated through her body.

Air sucked into her lungs and she coughed, throat aching and swollen, but breathing.

Bastian tossed aside a branch and bent over her.

"Tansy!" he gasped. "Are you alright?"

"Get up!" she rasped. "Might be more."

She coughed again, hoping the growing lump in her throat was something she could dislodge. It wasn't.

Bastian jumped up and pulled her to her feet, his eyes darting around. "Let's go," he said.

"Your—" she swallowed. "Your pack."

"Leave it," Bastian insisted. "Come on!"

Half dragging her by the hand he set off down the trail.

Tansy yanked her hand back, eyes wide as a loud, clambering rustle came from ahead. "What's that?" she whispered.

A tear leaked down her face as she reached for her knives. It wouldn't be enough, she knew. Her body ached, her throat burned, and she had run out of tricks.

"Bastian?" a voice called. "Tansy, are ye here? Where are—ack, what the fuck is that?"

"Garrett?" Bastian called out.

Tansy's tears ran freely now, and she sank against a tree, relief flooding her bones.

"AHH!" Garrett screamed. Tansy jumped, heart rate spiking again. "Get it off, get it OFF!" A quick scrambling noise ensued. "Fuck! That was the *biggest* fuckin' spider I've ever seen!"

A sob burst from Tansy's chest and she debated throwing one of her knives at the terrified rearick. When he finally emerged through the trees, though, she threw herself instead, wrapping her arms around him tightly. Then, she slapped him.

"What the fuck was that fer?" he yelped, pressing his hand to his stinging face.

Sharne and Carey arrived together, both with hands lazily resting on their weapons as they watched the exchange.

"A *SPIDER?*" Tansy yelled at him. "I thought you'd been attacked by a horde of flipping remnant!"

"Oh! Aye, about the remnant, ye see..." Garrett narrowed his eyes, finally noticing the bruise around her throat. "Oh, shite. Ye either already know, or young Bastian here needs a painful lesson on how to treat a lady."

"Hey!" Bastian squealed. "How could you even... I would never..."

"Untwist yer knickers, lad. I know ye wouldn't do that. And if ye, did, ye've learned yer lesson." Garrett sniggered.

Bastian raised a hand to his face where a purple bruise flourished beneath his touch. "You *knew* there were remnant?" Bastian asked.

Tansy whirled around to glare at Garrett.

"Well... I knew there *could* have been remnant," he admitted, backing away. "But we killed all the ones we saw, and then Bette was hurt, so I was—"

"What Garrett means to say," Sharne interrupted. "Is that he's very, very sorry for not sharing that vital information sooner, but he was so traumatized by the injury Bette sustained he wasn't thinking clearly."

"What? I didn't mean—" Garrett stopped when Sharne firmly tapped her hand on the back of his head. "Oh, fine. That's what I meant. Are ye both alright?"

Tansy nodded, her fury at Garrett fading as the reality sank in. "There might be one still alive. He's... well, he's stuck up a tree."

Garrett's eyes shot open at that, but she didn't let him speak.

"One accosted us at the ruins. He's dead. Then, two more found us on the trail. I snared one, he was dangling at the top of a sapling, but his screams stopped before we heard you. He's either fallen, or climbed down."

"And the other?" Carey asked, voice rich with concern.

"Dead," Tansy confirmed. "Bastian knocked him on the head."

"You're sure it killed him?" Sharne asked gently.

Tansy nodded, then winced as her throat muscles protested. "He looked dead, and he didn't complain when I cut his throat. So... I'm quite sure."

"Good, lass!" Garrett gushed. "I can't believe the two of ye fought three of the bastards off! And wee Bastian here without a lick of talent in 'im."

Garrett grinned widely, ignoring Bastian's offended glance.

"Can we go home now?" Tansy asked in a small voice. Her exhaustion pressed harder than her pride, and her breath still came in rasping gasps past the swelling in her windpipes.

"Aye," Garrett said. "We brought the horses, so ye don't have to walk."

Sharne wrapped an arm around Tansy gently. "You look beat to hell," the guard admitted as she helped her along.

Tansy mustered up a grin. "You should see the other guy."

"I have no doubt I will," Sharne said. "I don't imagine Garrett will let those bastards run around the forest freely."

Tansy gasped. "Surely you won't come back here?" she asked. "It's not safe!"

"It's not. But do you think they won't come for the town eventually?" Sharne shook her head. "We can't survive without trade, not this winter, and the traders won't come if they know there are remnant running about."

Tansy rested against Sharne as they walked. "I know," she said quietly. "I just... I've never seen one before. I didn't know they could be so vicious. And who is Chet?"

Sharne moved under Tansy's weight. "Chet?"

"Yeah," Tansy said, her mind drifting over her aches and pains, wondering how far they would have to walk to find the horses. "They kept talking about him, said he took the land after they were driven out by a monster."

"We'd best talk to Garrett about that," Sharne said. Then, looking down at the exhausted girl, suggested, "But maybe we'll wait until we're home, hey?"

CHAPTER TWENTY-ONE

Julianne regarded the three men trussed up on the ground before her.

"Hank," she said to the fourth trader. He squatted on the ground next to her. "I need you to tell me exactly what she said—or, as close as you can remember."

Hank's brow furrowed. "Filthy pigs, trying to turn a profit off those in need. Now, I'm going to profit off you. Kill the bitch. Don't let her pass. And don't speak to me again, you boor."

Julianne sighed. "There's nothing for it," she said. "I *have* to unwork the spell she put on them, there's no way around it."

Marcus groaned. "How long is that going to take?" he asked.

"Well, Hank's already done. Maybe an hour? Unless Artemis deigns to help." Julianne's eyes lit up as she delved into the mind of the second man, shaking off her irritation at her mystic companion.

Artemis had barely spoken since they had left his friends, apart from the occasional mumble about the unsatisfactory weather, the uncomfortable horse, or the long trip.

Marcus pulled a strand of grass and examined it, then nibbled it between his teeth. Hank sighed. Marcus stretched out. A fly buzzed overhead.

He lasted all of five minutes before he was up pacing again.

"You're distracting me," Julianne said pointedly. "I can put you to sleep, if you want."

With an irritable sigh, Marcus flopped back down on the ground. "I thought she wasn't as strong as Rogan," he muttered.

"She wasn't, not really. But she had the training of a full mystic, and she was powerful. Just… broken."

The active part of Julianne's mind drifted to a memory she had from inside Donna's mind, and she shuddered. Rogan wasn't just cruel; he was destructive. He had left gaping holes in Donna's mind.

"Actually, Rogan may have made her stronger," Julianne mused. "Either through his spellwork or his death." She paused, teasing out a snarled bit of mind control magic from her patient's mind.

"You'll have to explain," Marcus said. "Because I didn't think that was possible."

"The biggest dampener on anyone's magic is a natural aversion to pushing against our limits," Julianne said. "We can do it, but it's uncomfortable—for good reason. Push too hard and you burn yourself out."

"Like lifting a heavy weight?" Marcus asked. "A normal person can only lift so much, but if a child is crushed under a rock, we can push through that limit."

"Yes," Julianne said. "Ezekiel would compare it to a remnant mind. They have no natural limit. They will push harder and harder, past injury and damage, because they lack that aspect of their mind."

Marcus's face twisted into a grimace. "So, Donna is like a remnant now?"

Julianne shook her head. "Not really. And I can't say if this is even true—so far, it's just a theory. But she shouldn't have been able to use this level of power, even if she did know the mechanics."

"So, how do we combat that?" Marcus asked. "Could she be more powerful than you?"

Julianne shrugged. "Maybe. But if I'm right, and if she pushes that hard, she will burn out. That would be one end to the problem."

"And the other?" Marcus asked.

"I'll just have to kill her."

Julianne fell silent and let Marcus to dwell on her words. Of all the people Julianne had killed—and he had to admit, it was becoming quite a list—the ones that bothered her most were the mystics.

Those were the deaths that kept her up at night, that gave her nightmares and made her doubt herself. The mere thought of someone who shared the same gift she had, someone who could ignore the pain and suffering they caused and use that gift for evil, went against everything she believed in.

Marcus rolled over onto his side to watch her. Julianne sat quietly, eyes glossed over, hands gently resting on her knees. She couldn't have just killed the men, he knew. No, not her, he thought. She would do her best to save them, even if it meant letting Donna sneak even farther out of their reach.

"Done," she finally said.

"That took longer than expected," Marcus commented.

She arched an eyebrow. "All three of them," she clarified.

Marcus sat up, frowning. "You said it would take ages."

"I did." Julianne grinned. "But once I figured out a shortcut, it was much easier."

"Mental magic has shortcuts?" he asked.

Julianne chuckled. "Not really, but some spells have a specific neural pathway they follow. That makes them easy to study or replicate. Or, in this case, undo."

"I'll take your word for it," Marcus said, untying the three men. He gave the snoozing Artemis a nudge with his toe on the way past.

They set the traders on their way, once Julianne had given them all a brief check over.

"You're sure they won't have any nasty side effects?" Marcus asked, thinking back to some of the citizens of Tahn.

She shrugged. "Probably a nasty headache by morning. Maybe some disorientation, confusion. They should be fine in a day or two, and I planted a gentle suggestion in each of them to take it easy for a few days."

"You really do think of everything," Marcus grinned.

"It's my job," she sighed.

"Damn straight," Artemis snapped, coming up between them. "And I'm glad it's all hers and not mine." He jabbed his horse in the ribs and wandered ahead.

"What's wrong?" Marcus didn't have to see in her head to notice that as they drew nearer to the Temple, her mood was dropping.

Julianne mustered up a brave smile. "Nothing."

Marcus yanked on his reins, bringing his horse to a stop. Warily, Julianne tugged on Cloud's, too.

"Look," he said. "I know you're important. You're a leader, and you'll be busy and have secrets, and you won't always have time for me. But Julianne... I want to make this work. I can't do that if you're not honest with me."

"I can't promise to tell you everything," she pleaded.

He shook his head. "I'm not asking for that. I've worked around higher-ups long enough to know there are some things that can't be shared." He nudged the horse over, so he could look her in the eye. "But don't say you're fine when you're not."

She dropped her gaze. "I'm sorry. I guess I was trying so hard to ignore it that I didn't want to admit I was lying to myself, too." She took a deep breath. "Marcus, I'm going to be so busy when I get back! There will be people around all the time, asking me for things, usually not with their mouths."

He reached a hand out and touched her knee. "We'll be ok," he said. "We can make time. Little snatches, here and there. I won't make you choose between me and the Temple."

Giving him a wobbly smile, Julianne put her hand on his. "Thank you. Next time I'm being stupid, don't wait so long to point it out?"

"Oh, that's a promise I can keep." Marcus laughed and set off again. "Let's see if we can't hit Craigston by nightfall at least. Race you!"

They rode as fast as their horses could comfortably maintain, quickly catching up to Artemis and not slowing until the road began to creep upwards and the horses started to snort and huff. Drawing in to a walk, they trudged up the mountain.

"We're not going to beat the sun," Julianne said, eyeing the long shadows.

Marcus nodded in agreement. "Too dangerous to camp halfway up, though," he said. "Once the light drops, we'll walk. We can stop in Craigston for the night and head up to the Temple first thing. That is, if you're not too tired?"

His tone was loaded with a challenge, and Julianne snorted. "I'm not the one who whined about a blistered foot for three days after a hunting trip back in Tahn," she reminded him.

"Oh, that smarts." Marcus said. "You're never going let me to live that down, are you?"

Julianne shook her head eagerly. "Did you think I would? You had Annie running about after you like you'd lost a damn leg!"

"It hurt!" he protested.

"It was a grass injury," Julianne said with a laugh.

"If you ever have a clump stuck in your shoe for six hours, let me know how you do," he grumped back.

"Whatever, tough-guy." Julianne stuck her tongue out and nudged Cloud a little faster up the mountain.

They made good time, only dismounting a mile short of Craigston—though, that was still too soon for Artemis. The moonlight was bright and clear, lighting their way along the mountain road, so he stayed on his horse and let Julianne lead it along the narrow path.

"Who goes?" a call rang out through the quiet evening.

"Julianne, Temple Master," she called. "And two others."

"Ye've a hide comin' back here," the voice snarled. A short man stomped over to them, hands on hips as he glared up at Julianne.

"Oh, Bitch's oath," she muttered under her breath. Then, louder, "I haven't set foot in Craigston for some months. Are you saying otherwise?"

"Fuckin' mental dickbags. Between you twats and the bandits, this shit is just gettin' old." The rearick turned, then gestured over his shoulder. "I suppose ye'll just mind-fuck me if I try keep ye out, so I may as well take ye ta Tavich."

"I think that would be best," Julianne agreed. Then, her eyes flashed white as she sent to the others. *This doesn't sound good. If Donna has damaged the relationship between Craigston and the Temple, I'll wring her damn neck. Keep your heads down, and for Bitch's sake, Artemis, be polite!*

I'm always *polite*, Artemis sent back. *Master.* The sarcasm dripped from his thoughts, and she debated leaving him to wait outside.

Marcus surrendered his weapon at the rearick's request. "There are knives in my bags, too," he offered. "And a magitech rifle, but it has no amphorald."

The rearick nodded thanks, but waved off Marcus's offer to hand the extra weapons over. "I'm no' stupid. That one there could take half this town before anyone blinked, if the rumors about 'er are true."

"You'll find there's often more smoke than fire when it comes to rumors," Julianne noted dryly.

"I don't plan on stickin' my hand in ta find out, either way." The rearick led them to a little cottage just down from Ophelia's. Like the rest of the town, it was dusted with coal and soot from the mines.

Julianne nodded her thanks as the rearick rapped on the door three times, then stood back.

The door flung open to reveal Tavich standing with a scowl on his face, wearing flimsy cotton pajamas. "You!" he growled.

"She says she's not," their guide remarked.

Tavich lifted a bushy eyebrow. "Send for the guard." He stood silently as the other rearick dashed off, then stepped back inside.

"Tavich, I'm sorry to have disturbed you. It seems someone has been through Craigston since my last visit, posing as me." Julianne sat at the little table, hands folded.

Tavich thumped into a chair next to her, face glowering. There were only two chairs, so Marcus stood awkwardly by the door with Artemis. "And how do we know what's real?" he asked. "All yer mystics parade through here, usin' yer magic on us like we're dogs ta be used fer training. Magic users've been through here and have made a few friends by savin' a few lives, but they didn't use that mind shit. I still don't trust it, but I trust it more than I do you."

He spat on the floor, and Marcus's hand went to his side, forgetting for a moment that he wasn't armed.

"I'm sorry," Julianne said. "The relationship between the mystics and the rearick has always been friendly—I would hate for that to end now. I have done nothing to cause that to happen."

"So, me men are alive?" Tavich asked with an accusing tone.

"Bette and Garrett? They're fine. A rural lord offered them a chance to lead a small army in defense of a growing town, and they took it." Julianne sighed. "Look, I crossed the Madlands months ago. I haven't been back this side of them until the last couple of days, and didn't step foot on the Heights until this afternoon."

"Even if that were so, do ye have *any* idea what we've been through here? Bandits robbin' and killin' my men. Good, honest rearick dyin' on their way to Arcadia with the amphoralds. We've been considerin' puttin' a stop ta the trips, but fer now, we need the coin. Now, after that, we have all this with the damn mystics. We've found some remnant sniffin' around the area again, too. It's been hell since ye've been gone. And now ye claim ye ain't been back 'til taday, eh?"

Julianne's eyes widened. She had no idea all that had been happening. Bandits here, too? What did that mean? And they were after the amphorald crystals? Unless they had engineers, those wouldn't do them a bit of good. She wondered if Amelia was aware of the situation, but then promptly shut that down when she realized she must be. There was no way the shipments were being taken without her knowledge.

Clearing her throat and pushing all her questions aside, she decided to stick with the problem that arose right now. "Yes. That's right. I've met several people on my way back that claimed to have seen me before, which was impossible because I took a different path upon returning than I did when crossing through. I know it's difficult to believe or hear, but today truly is my first day back on the mountain."

"Show me yer hire papers," Tavich barked.

Someone tapped on the door and pushed it open, passing through a leather satchel. Marcus immediately recognized it as Julianne's.

Guess they did grab my weapons after all, he mused, confident the presentation of Bette and Garrett's hire agreement would convince Tavich of what he needed to know.

Tavich passed the bag to Julianne and waited while she rustled through it. After a moment, she looked up, her eyes meeting Marcus's, face white. "It's not here," she said quietly. Suddenly standing, she dumped the contents of the bag at her feet. A sprinkle of fine white dust puffed out.

"Bitch-Damn it," she cursed. "Where do my papers keep disappearing to?"

Artemis snorted. "You're a mystic, just make him think you have them."

Tavich's face flushed a deep shade of red. "How dare ye?" he sputtered. "How dare ye come into my town after what ye've done."

"I haven't done *anything*," Julianne protested. "I'm sorry for my colleague—I wouldn't dream of—"

"*GUARDS!*" Tavich had barely finished bellowing when six heavily armed rearick busted open the door and trotted inside, angry faced and weapons at the ready.

"Ye will escort these traitorous filth to the cells. Lock 'em up, not together. Send word to the Temple we have their leader—if that's even who she is." Tavich walked up to Julianne, jabbing a finger into her chest. "And if ye even fart magic, I'll destroy every treaty we have and burn them beneath yer feet as ye scream fer mercy."

Julianne swallowed, but bowed her head in deference. Outsiders might assume Tavich was nothing more than a businessman, but she knew that to the rearick, his rank was equal to hers.

Marcus's mind raced as he opened his shields to Julianne, but she didn't dive into his mind or send him any messages. He fell back on her earlier words—be polite.

Despite his instincts screaming for him not to, he followed her lead, holding out his hands to be tied. Artemis did the same, with a pleasant expression that Marcus was sure would turn into an 'I told you so' tirade as soon as he had the chance.

The guards led them to a small, dismal building hewn out of the rock. Three heavy iron gates were carefully unlocked, the keys attached to the first guard's belt with a thick chain.

A row of cells lined the walls after the third gate, lit by flickering lanterns that did little to dispel the shadows this deep in the mountain.

Julianne was thrust into the first cell. The guards dragged Marcus down to shove him into a small room beside her.

Once Artemis was secured in a third cell, the guards filed out the door, slamming it shut before keys jangled in the lock. A loud click made Marcus's heart sink as the thump of boots on stone faded away.

"Everyone ok?" Marcus called.

"Peachy," Artemis snapped. "Just peachy."

"I'm fine, Marcus," Julianne said with a sigh. "They didn't hurt me."

"What now?" he asked, sure that Julianne had a plan.

"We wait," she said. "Best get some sleep. I'm not sure what morning will hold, but it will be easier to face if we're clear-headed."

"Ha!" Artemis barked loudly, then fell silent.

"Julianne, tell me you have a plan to get out of here?" Marcus begged. "Was I supposed to do something back there? I could have fought them, but—"

"No!" Julianne stressed the word. "You shouldn't have done that. Marcus, remember when you said you knew that sometimes I wouldn't be able to share things with you? For the sake of the Temple?"

"Yeah," Marcus said dubiously.

"This is one of those times. I have to ask you to trust me, but I can't tell you what's going to happen. Just that we must preserve the relationship between mystics and rearick." Marcus heard a sigh, one loaded with the weight of responsibility.

"Ok." Marcus stifled his own heaving sigh—one of frustration. "I trust you. Just tell me what you need me to do."

"Just..." Julianne paused, and he imagined her biting her lip. "Go with the flow, and try not to kill anyone. And also try to get some sleep."

"Bitch help me," Marcus muttered as he rolled over, pulling his coat tightly around him. "This is going to be an interesting couple of days."

CHAPTER TWENTY-TWO

Bastian yelped as Polly pressed the wet cloth to his face.

"Oh, for goodness sake," she snapped. "Man up; it's just a graze."

"Easy for you to say," Bastian grumbled.

"Go and ask your girlfriend how many times she whined about her wounds. She was a lot worse off than you are," Polly said pointedly.

Bastian's cheeks flamed. "She's not my girlfriend!" He winced, then sighed. "Sorry. I'm just not used to this sort of stuff."

"You? You crossed the Madlands! Danil told us all how together you fought off hordes of remnant, fighting for your lives." Polly's eyes were wide and excited.

"Danil?" Bastian snorted. "He wasn't even conscious for half the trip. Did he leave that out?"

Polly's mouth flattened. "Perhaps he did, the sneaky bastard. No matter. It still must have been dangerous. Is Tahn making you soft?" she teased.

Bastian smiled. "I was born soft, and I'll die soft. I've given up trying to compete with the others—fighting isn't my strong point."

Polly grinned. "That's ok," she said. "You've got other talents. Do you think it will be long until your school opens?"

Bastian groaned. "Years. Decades, even, the way things are going!"

Polly frowned, her finely shaped eyebrows drawing together with only a delicate pucker between them. "Why?"

"You didn't hear? The site I wanted to use has been infested with remnant." He heaved a disappointed sigh. "With those monsters running around the countryside, I'm not even sure a school is a good idea."

Polly clicked her tongue. "Don't be silly. You know Garrett won't let them just wander freely—he'll hunt them down, wipe them out and make your little plot of land nice and safe."

Bastian turned woeful eyes up to her as she removed the cloth and nodded, happy that the wound would heal on its own. "You think so?"

"I'm as sure of that as I am of my own name." She winked. "And I'm as sure of *that* as if I'd picked it myself… which I did, by the way. Imagine growing up to be called Gertrude? Ridiculous."

Bastian snorted. "Gertrude? You're joking, right?"

She shook her head primly. "And if I ever go back to that godforsaken little farm in the middle of bumfuck nowhere, I'll tell them what a horrible idea it was."

"You haven't seen your parents in a while, then?"

Polly shook her head. "We come from a little village—well, it's not even that, really. It's doesn't have a name, but there's a little cluster of five families way up past Muir. Beautiful area, even if it'll kill you dead in the wintertime."

"Wow," Bastian said. "I didn't even know there were towns out this far before we crossed over the Madlands." He blushed, realizing how backwards that sounded. "I mean, I knew there were towns, of course… I just didn't expect it to be so much *bigger* than home."

Polly grinned. "And people wonder why Danil and I want to go and explore it."

The smile fell from Bastian's face. "Danil's... leaving?"

Polly's eyes shot open and a hand flew to her mouth. "Oh, damn, he hasn't told you? Bastian, I'm so sorry."

He shook his head, fighting off disappointment. "No, it's ok. I mean, Danil doesn't owe us anything. He's a grown man and can do what he wants."

Polly rested a hand on his shoulder. "It won't be for a while. He's determined to stay until you're well on your way to setting up the school. He said he might even be able to send some students your way."

I need to get my hands on another amphorald, Bastian thought. *I can't do this alone. Losing Julianne was bad enough...*

Seeing his crestfallen expression, Polly flew into a motherly tizz. "Oh, Bastian. You won't be left alone." Polly leaned down to hug him, her bosom pressing against his face. "The people of Tahn adore you. They'll look after you."

"Bitch take me, Bastian! Why is your face in my girlfriend's chest?" Danil's angry voice filled the room.

Bastian shot back, heart screaming into his mouth, sore muscles shrieking at the sudden movement. "I didn't—I'm sorry!" he gasped.

A moment later his wits returned enough to see Danil leaning over a chair, almost doubled over in wheezing laughter. Polly walked over and slapped the back of his head.

"That was mean!" she snapped. Then, she hit him again. "*And* you were supposed to tell Bastian about leaving weeks ago!"

That sobered Danil quickly. "Ah, shit. You know?" he asked.

Still reeling at the sudden changes in Danil's demeanor, Bastian scowled. "You're an ass, Danil."

"I agree, but which particular asshole act are we referring to?" Danil asked, sitting down at the table. "Just so we're clear."

"All of them!" Bastian exclaimed. "Why didn't you say anything?"

"I thought it would just make you worry more. Bitch knows you already do enough of that for the two of us." Danil reached over to grab Polly's hand and tug her onto his lap. When she sat, he kissed her cheek.

"You still could have warned me," Bastian said.

Danil shrugged. "I should have. I'm sorry, Bastian." Danil narrowed his eyes. "Let me make it up to you."

"Oh, no," Bastian walked over to the door. "If you really mean it, don't do anything to prove it. No spontaneous parties, no madcap plans, nothing. Promise?"

Danil let out a snort. "No! As if I'd ever promise that."

Bastian rolled his eyes. "You're incorrigible. I'm starting to realize why Julianne wanted to leave you behind."

"Hey!" Danil called as Bastian disappeared. "She never said that!"

Bastian blinked, eyes adjusting to the fading light. He realized he had nowhere to be. Plans for the school would now grind to a halt, until he found a new location, or the remnant had been thoroughly rousted from the area.

Thinking of the unexpected attack, he decided to go and see Bette. He wouldn't burden her with the issue, but perhaps she had already been told. If anyone would have a plan to kill some dirty remnant, it was Bette.

He tapped on a window of the cottage shared by the two rearick. Inside, a lantern bobbed as it was brought to the door. It swung open and Garrett peered out, his beard dimming the light in his hand.

"Ah, yer all patched up?" Garrett asked, seeing Bastian.

"Yes," he said, "Though I might need to bribe Mathias for a heal in the morning. Bastard's balls, my muscles are aching."

"Aye, ye'll find that'll hurt like a bitch tomorrow." Garrett ushered him inside. "Come and say hello to me lass."

"She's awake?" Bastian hovered at the door suddenly having second thoughts.

"Aye, and in a right foul mood. Don't think yer gettin' out of it, lad. Ye're here, so yer gonna go in there an' talk to 'er." Garrett pushed Bastian towards the hall.

"That bad?" Bastian asked.

"Aye. She's a right cow while she's stuck in that damned bed, but Mary says she's not ta leave it at least 'til morning."

With one last mighty push, Garrett shoved a stumbling Bastian into a small, brightly lit room at the back of the cottage.

"Bastian!" Bette exclaimed. "Have ye come ta smuggle me out, then?" she whispered loudly.

"I heard that, woman!" Garrett yelled from the next room. "An' he's a good lad. Wouldn't risk losing his balls ta old Mary, not fer you."

Bastian shrugged. "He's right," he admitted. "Mary feeds me, so I'm not about to piss her off."

Bette's gleeful smile dissolved into a frown. "Ye prick. Fine, then. What do ye want?"

"I just came to say hi." Bastian raised his hands defensively and backed towards the door. "I'm sorry! I didn't mean to bother you."

"Och, sit down ye precious wee thing." Bette patted the bed with one hand. "I know I'm a grouchy old nag, but if I don't have someone ta talk to other than that old goat out there, I'll go madder than a remnant!"

Bastian tentatively sat on the end of the crisply tucked sheets. "So… how do you feel?" he asked, wondering if it was the wrong question.

"Bloody well fine," Bette heaved. "Achin' ta go kill those bastard runts that did that ta yer face," she said, nodding at the scrape on Bastian's cheek.

"They're mostly dead, I think," Bastian said. "There were only three—Tansy killed two of them, Garrett got the one she stranded up a tree."

Bette hooted with laughter. "Aye, he told me about her little trick. Clever lass! Yer lucky she went with ye!"

Bastian shuddered, realizing for the first time how lucky he was that she had seen him ready to sneak out without her. "I'd be dead if not for her."

"Aye, ye would!" Bette said happily. "Now, I'll bet me ass that there are more of the beasts out there. Between the three ye saw and that Chet fellow they were rantin' about, *and* the thieves Garrett caught, who said the remnant rousted them out of their home…"

Impatient fingers drummed the bedspread as Bette's eyes twinkled. "Aye, a mighty fight we'll be up for! We'll lead a patrol and hunt the remnant down, we will, and I'll get me vengeance fer this bloody thing." She waved a bandaged arm, then winced.

"You should be careful with that," Bastian said, then clamped his mouth shut as she glowered.

"I've done nothing but be bloody careful fer days! What do they think I am, a bloody porcelain doll?" Bette huffed, blowing a tendril of hair away from her face. "Ach. Never mind that. How is Tansy?"

"She's ok," Bastian said. "A little banged up, but Mathias fixed her up." He cocked his head, suddenly realizing something. "Why hasn't—"

"Don't ye even say it!" Bette snapped. "He's a lovely man and all, but he can keep his Bitch-cursed magic to himself, thank you."

Bastian's eyebrows raised, surprised. "I thought you didn't mind magic use?"

"I don't," Bette confirmed. "As long as its use is directed somewhere other than me."

Bastian shook his head in awe of her stubbornness. "He could have you fixed up in a few heartbeats," he pointed out.

Bette screwed up her face even harder. "It's nothing a few days won't fix," she said. "And scars make ye tougher!"

Bastian winced at the thought of putting up with a gaping shoulder wound for a week or more when a druid was right down the lane, ready to help. He knew Bette wouldn't see it that way, but he wondered if he could change her mind.

"Ok," he said, standing to go. "I'd best go see Francis, make sure the curfew is being held and the travel restrictions are in place."

"Curfew?" Bette sat up, despite the sharp look of pain that shot across her face as she moved. "What travel restrictions?"

Bastian shook his head sadly. "Well, you can't expect him to let people wander about with deranged beasts running about. It's not safe! Without you to protect us, and Garrett so worried about—"

"Bullshit," Bette said, throwing off her blanket and swinging her legs of the bed.

Bastian jumped up, hands raised, unsure whether it was worth the risk to his life to try and manhandle her back to bed. "Garrett?" he called in a wavering voice.

The quick clump of feet rang, and Garrett burst in. "What the bloody hell did ye do to her?" he screeched. "Get back to yer bed, lass!"

"Fuck off!" Bette snapped. "I've got a druid to see."

She shambled past him, cupping her bad arm while trying to keep it still as she walked.

"How the bloody hell did ye convince her ta see Mathias?" Garrett whispered.

Bastian shrugged. "I just told her how much we needed her."

Garrett slid a narrowed glance Bastian's way, then ushered him out. "Off ye go. Give the druid some warning he's about ta be accosted by an angry woman, lad."

Bastian waited until Bette was clear of the door. As she

stopped a moment to catch her breath, he slipped past, running for Mathias's tent.

"Ye bastard," Bette grunted. "Why didn't ye tell me the town was under curfew? And travel restrictions? Tahn will starve if we don't hurry up and trade for winter."

"Curfew?" Garrett asked. Then, realizing, he nodded. "Aye, the curfew. Very serious, that curfew. Must be keepin' the people safe."

Bette spared a suspicious glance his way, then continued her ambling progress to the door. By the time she stepped onto the road, Rhea had run to collect her.

Bette jerked back. "Oh, no. Not a bastard chance, I'm not havin' no apprentice work on me!"

Rhea laughed. "I'm just here to watch and help. No magic, just fluffing pillows." She hailed the druid who was making his way through the dark streets towards them. "Over here, Matti!"

"Matti?" Bette whispered to Garrett. "How bloody long was I in that room?"

"Bette, I could have come to you, you know," Mathias gently admonished. "Here, don't go too far. We can do the healing here."

"In the middle of the bloody road?" Bette protested.

"We can go back to your room if you prefer?" He raised a slender eyebrow.

"Middle of the road is just fine," she grunted. "Hurry up. And no dickin' about." She hesitated, then said, "And not too much. I don't want the scar ta be gone, if ye understand me?"

Mathias winked and grinned as his eyes lit up, a green glow softly shining in the darkness. Bette sucked in a shuddering gasp, squeezed her eyes shut and held her breath. Mathias's eyes cleared.

He waited. Bette still stood, face puckered, straining for breath. "Hurry up," she squeaked.

"Hurry up?" he asked casually.

"Yes!" Her eyes shot open as a rush of air left her lungs. "What're ye waiting for?"

He shrugged. "It's done."

"It's not—oh." She flexed her arm and peeled the blood-encrusted linen shirt off it, peeking in. "Oh! Ye did a bloody good job."

She pulled the shirt down, scrubbing at the blood staining her skin so Garrett could see a shiny knot of scar tissue protruding from the healed wound. "*Ohh*! That looks hideous!" she squealed happily.

"Aye," Garrett said, smiling softly. "A true warrior's mark, that one. Not that ye need it in me eyes, love."

"Aww, ye wee darlin'." Bette leaned in with her lips pursed, but Garrett jerked back.

"Would ye stop calling me that! There's only a few inches difference between us!" he yelled.

"Ye vain prick, yer shorter than me, so yer *wee*. That's how it works, ye numpty!"

Mathias bowed. "I'll leave you two to discuss matters of height. I'm off to bed."

Both rearick watched in shock as Rhea slipped her arm through Mathias's, gave them a cheeky wave, and walked off into the darkness with him.

"When the bloody hell did that happen?" Garrett asked.

"Fucks me," Bette said. "I'm not surprised, though. He's quite tall. Ladies like that." Garrett whirled on her, and she burst into giggles. "Yer lucky I'm no lady, me love."

"Women!" He threw his hands up in the air and stomped back home.

CHAPTER TWENTY-THREE

Marcus shot to his feet when something rustled, hand once again searching for a weapon he didn't have. There was a scrape of metal on metal, and the outer prison door swung open.

Marcus jumped up to peer out the small hatch in his cell door, but couldn't see anything except the wall across from him.

"Who's there?" he demanded.

"Gus. Where's the lady?" a gruff voice answered.

Be careful, Jules, Marcus thought, hoping that by some chance she was in his head. *He may not be who he says he is.*

"I'm over here," Julianne said. "What are you doing down this way, Gus?" she asked cheerfully.

"Gettin' yer ass out of the lockup. Not right what Tavich did, not right at all."

Metal clinked again, then Marcus heard the snick of a lock opening. A creak sounded as a shadow passed the tiny window at his door.

"Thank you, Gus. Do you have all the keys there?" Julianne asked.

Gus mumbled an affirmative, and Marcus heard a jangle. A moment later, Julianne's face appeared, grinning. "Looks like I'm saving your ass once again, dear." Another snick, and his door swung open.

"Pretty sure this one is down to Gus," Marcus pointed out, shaking the rearick's hand in thanks. He watched Julianne slip the key into a third door. "Do we really have to let him out?"

"Shut your mouth, or next time you see your girlfriend naked, you'll start thinking about your mother," Artemis called from inside his cell.

"Artemis! You do that and I'll have you walking around the Temple nude for a week," Julianne snapped, yanking his door open.

"Ha! You think that would worry me?" Artemis cackled, standing to brush off his wrinkled robes.

Julianne arched an eyebrow. "No. But it wouldn't worry Esme, either, or a few of the other older women. You'd have all their attention."

Artemis's face fell. "Bah. Fine. You won this round, but if you don't keep his manners in check, don't you complain about mine."

"Manners be damned," Gus said in a low voice, handing a bundle to Marcus. "If ye don't all shut yer mouths, ye'll be back in those cells and me with ye!"

Artemis grunted, but fell silent. Julianne winked at Marcus as he strapped his weapons back on.

"Thank you," he mouthed.

Next time, don't antagonize him, Julianne sent back.

Marcus bit back a reply, but Julianne grinned, already having seen the snarky comment float through his thoughts.

When we get to the Temple, she sent, *make sure you're shielded to everyone but me. Hell, even shield me if that makes you more secure.*

What if you need me? Marcus thought.

I'll give your shields a shove, Julianne replied. *You're getting really good at noticing that.*

Gus led the way out of the dank, damp prison, unlocking each of the doors with one of the cluster of keys jangling from a large, rusty ring. Marcus itched to know where he had gotten it, but didn't risk speaking aloud.

Gus held a hand up as they approached the last door. Light flickered through the window grate on this one, and when Gus thrust the key in noisily, someone cried out in alarm.

"Shut yer trap, Marrick, it's just me," Gus snapped.

"What are ye doin' down there?" Marrick asked. "Bastard's oath, Gus, yer not down there with a lass, are ye? After all the strife ye were in last time—"

Something thudded, and Marrick fell silent. Gus waggled his fingers, gesturing the others through.

Marcus peered in first, spotting Marrick unconscious in the corner with a red welt on his head. As he passed, Marcus gave a sympathetic grimace. Gus caught his look and chuckled.

"He's had worse from his Ma after a hard night at Ophelia's."

Julianne shook her head with a sigh, but a small smile tugged at her lips.

Gus tipped his head to her. "Master Julianne, I don't suppose ye could use that magic stuff ta disguise yerself?" He waggled his fingers, and Marcus wondered if he had ever really seen a mystic cast before. "Not on me, mind," he added with a shiver.

"Scared?" Marcus teased, then thought better of it when Gus nodded.

"I'll never forget that day on the mountain. Not right, thinkin' yer friends are bandits and not right tryin' ta kill 'em, either." Gus's bushy brow furrowed, and he chewed his whiskers. "Any rate, let's be goin'. Just follow me, there's an easier way to get back than the one ye know. And don't be seen!"

"Stay close, gentlemen, and quiet," Julianne said quietly, her eyes shifting to a solid white glow.

Gus opened the door, and a gust of wind blew in, bringing a few stray snowflakes with it.

"Jules, if we leave footprints can you mask them?" Marcus asked.

She shook her head. "Not for long. Be careful where you step."

"If we get caught, run," Artemis said. "I'll cover your escape. Don't turn back and don't come for me."

Marcus opened his mouth to protest, but caught Julianne's stern nod.

They won't hurt him, she reassured Marcus. *Once we get back to the Heights and roust Donna out, we can patch things up with Tavich.*

Another fluffy swirl of snowflakes gusted past as they stepped outside, and Marcus was dismayed to see the dark, hard packed dirt of Craigston speckled with white tufts and slippery patches of frozen ground.

"Go slow," Julianne warned Gus. "We'll need to be careful where we step."

Gus frowned, but walked off towards the back of Craigston, his followers behind him dancing between patches of dry ground. Around them, Craigston bustled despite the late hour.

"Where are you taking us?" Julianne asked in a low voice.

Mumbling into his beard, Gus explained. "There's a huntin' trail out past the amphorald mine. If ye follow it, it goes way up the mountain and comes out near yer Temple."

"And no one mentioned it to us?" Julianne asked pointedly.

Gus shrugged. "Rearick's gotta have his secrets."

Marcus watched a train of workers head away from the mines towards Ophelia's bar. Skin smudged with dark dirt, and hair and beards frizzed in the crisp weather, they looked exhausted, but satisfied after a hard day's work.

"Should'a waited until the evenin' shift was home," Gus muttered under his breath.

"Wozzat? Gus!" one of the workers yelled. "What ye doin' out this late?"

"Business!" Gus yelled back tersely.

"Just because ye pay yer girlfriend for her love, don't make it a business!" the rearick yelled back, causing hoots of laughter from those around him.

"Go fuck yerself," Gus called, eyes darting worriedly around to the three people behind him.

"What, ye got that itch in yer ballsack again, ye cranky old bastard?"

"Shut up!" Gus yelled, nostrils flaring.

"Easy now," Marcus said in a low voice. "We're avoiding attention, not looking for it."

It was too late. A gang of miners swaggered over, all clamoring to know what kind of condition might affect a man's nether regions so badly it turned him into a dick to his friends.

"I'm just going for a fuckin' walk! Nothin' ta see," Gus said. "Not unless yer wantin' to hold me dick while I take a piss in the bushes."

"Traitor!" The loud yell came from the direction of the jail. "The prisoners escaped! Mystics on the loose!"

"Oh, shit," Gus muttered. "Go!" he yelled directly at Marcus. "I'll be fine, just get her home!" He jerked his head towards Julianne, then turned to meet the crowd of rearick who watched the exchange, suspicion growing.

Marcus grabbed Julianne's arm. He reached for Artemis, but the old man jerked back, eyes glowing. "I'll meet you there, boy."

Then, a deep, booming voice reverberated in his skull. *Let the Master be hurt, and I'll tie your balls to a string and make you jerk it every time you blink.*

"Bitch's oath," Marcus muttered. "Get the fuck out of my head, you old grump!"

He tugged Julianne, and they set off running. Behind them, the sound of an explosion from deep in the mine sent up screams of fear.

"Was that real?" Marcus said, feeling the blood drain from his face.

"No," Julianne muttered. "They won't be fooled for long." She cast an agonized glance over her shoulder, the lapse in concentration leading her to slip on the icy ground.

She went sprawling, and Marcus, still latched onto her arm, went with her. They skidded over a small embankment and tumbled down a hill, sharp branches slicing at their skin as they rolled over bushes and underbrush.

"Oh, shit!" Marcus gasped as they came to a stop. He looked around, barely able to see past the deep shadows. "Jules, are you ok?"

"I'm fine," she said, voice shaking.

Marcus quickly reached out for her hand, tugging her to her feet. When she cried out in pain, he dropped it. "What is it?" he asked urgently.

"Nothing," she said. "Just my arm. It'll be fine."

Marcus peered up the hill. Pinpoints of light wavered, growing brighter. "They're coming after us," he said. Then, a rush of fire at the top of the hill whooshed upwards, crackling trees and filling the air with smoke.

"Another illusion?" he asked.

Julianne frowned. "Yes, but…" A line of flame raced down the mountain towards them. "That's real."

"What?" Marcus helped her to stand, and she leaned on him as they hobbled away.

"There was a small fire. Artemis must have made it look bigger, but parts are real." She pointed up towards the source with one hand, cradling the other across her middle. "We have to get up there, find the path Gus told us about."

Marcus drew his sword and wrapped the other arm around Julianne. "Come on, then!"

They awkwardly made their way uphill as the fire grew. Marcus coughed, and Julianne covered her face with the edge of her robe. Ahead, screams and yells combined into an urgent plea for help to fight the rapidly growing flames as others yelled for the guard.

"They're up the hill! Get them!" someone yelled.

"I hope that's a trick," Marcus rasped.

Julianne nodded, her eyes still white. Though the smoke now blew away from them and the flames seemed to be dying a little, tears streamed down her face. "Artemis has Gus hidden in Tavich's house."

"What?" Marcus yelped. "He's an idiot!"

Julianne shook her head. "Genius. He'll be able to disguise them there until the excitement dies down. Then they can sneak out." Her face tightened, and she muttered, "If you don't sneak out, I'll come get you myself, you old coot."

Marcus stopped, letting Julianne rest on a tree for a moment. They were almost at the top of the hill.

"There's a *lot* of people out there, Jules."

She sucked in a deep breath, her face slackening. Marcus was familiar with the procedure. Julianne had slipped into a trance, not one of magic, but one that centered her mind and calmed her thoughts.

"I've got this," she said.

The trail they had run down was full of people. Julianne directed Marcus into the center of it. *If we bump into someone, they won't notice if there are heaps of people around,* she explained.

Marcus nodded, still holding her close as they wove through rearick. Someone jostled Julianne, and she gasped in pain. When Marcus looked to see if they were noticed, it was another rearick who bore the brunt of the irritated glare.

Faces swam around them as buckets were passed and terse orders shouted just inches away from Marcus's ears. His feet were kicked, and he tripped, body thrown about like a leaf in storm water as rearick shoved him to and fro.

Julianne pulled a little away from Marcus. With her ability to mind read, she could predict the movements of those around them, sometimes nudging a rearick out of their way by making them take a step to one side. As they moved forward, bodies pressed in behind them.

Marcus stayed silent, mirroring Julianne's movements as she darted left, took two steps forward, ducked right, and stepped back to let a stocky man with a bucket lunge past.

Finally, they broke free, stepping out into air that was still smoky, but no longer bore the odor of fresh sweat and old dust. Behind them, rearick shouted in victory as the last of the fire was smothered.

"Hurry," Julianne said, stumbling forwards. "I can't hold this spell much longer."

Marcus leaned down and carefully scooped her up, nestling her against his chest to immobilize the arm he suspected was broken. She gave a low cry of pain, then settled into him.

"Go," she whispered.

Marcus took long strides, keeping his movements steady as he walked quickly along the path. He slowed as fresh ice covered the path, quickening his pace again when it cleared. Overhead, snow began to fall again, sparse flakes brushing his face and shoulders.

Julianne shivered, and he gently tightened his grip, pressing her against his chest. The exertion of carrying her uphill flushed his skin, banishing the cold from his bones and helping to keep her warm.

He crept around a narrow corner, then slowed as the trail sloped steeply uphill. "Jules? Jules, are you still with me?"

Marcus looked down. Julianne's eyes were closed, her face pale and breathing shallow. He glared up the mountain at a trail that seemed impossible to climb with no idea how much farther he had to travel.

"Best place for you is at the Temple," he grunted, panting. "So, no stopping. But I need you to stay with me, ok?"

She murmured something softly in her sleep and Marcus took it as an affirmative. "Right, then. No stopping. Bitch's oath, I hate mountains."

CHAPTER TWENTY-FOUR

Bastian twitched in his sleep, twisting at the blankets, one arm curled up awkwardly against his chest.

"Put me down," he mumbled. "I can walk."

Someone banged on his door, and he shot upright, sweat beading on his forehead. He stretched out his arm, rubbing away a cramp in his bicep. "Damn," he muttered. "That was a really shitty dream."

He had been lying on the side of a mountain, arm hurt. Then, someone had plucked him up and carried him away, jostling the sore arm. Snow had lashed his skin, chilling him. He pulled the blankets up to his chin, sleep creeping back through the darkness to lull him into a relaxed snooze.

Bang, bang, bang.

"Shit!" Bastian jumped up again, remembering what had woken him so abruptly the first time. He raced down the narrow stairs and yanked the door open, squinting into the first rays of dawn.

Garrett leaned on the door jamb, sword at his hip, scratching his beard.

"Garrett? What's wrong?" Bastian's heart jumped into his

throat, wondering what crisis had brought the rearick to his door at this early hour.

Without thinking, Bastian's eyes went white as he slipped into the rearick's head, ready to grab any vital information about the impending emergency.

He saw Garrett's intent and groaned. A moment later, he slammed the door shut and stomped away.

"Hey! That's no welcome fer someone come ta help ye out, ye prick!"

"You came for breakfast, you greedy hog," Bastian called back, hesitating with one foot on the stairs.

"I can't deny a good feed *was* on me mind, but I'm here ta help yer school. If ye don't wanna hear it…" Garrett's voice trailed away.

Bastian sighed, warring for a moment with his desire to climb back into bed. He knew he wouldn't be able to sleep, though, so he went back to the door and fumbled it open.

He pointed to the kitchen. "There's a cold box with some bacon and maybe two eggs left. The pan is in that cupboard, and the fire starter is in that drawer."

Garrett grinned happily. "Sit yer ass down, ye lazy shit. I'll cook fer all of us!"

"All of us?" Bastian asked, before suddenly remembering the last time Garrett had been allowed to prepare food. "Uh, you know what? I'll do breakfast. It will help wake me up."

He chased Garrett out of the kitchen, and when someone knocked at the door, he sent the rearick to open it.

"Good mornin', Bastian!" Bette called, striding in with a woven bag on one arm. "Och, sit yerself down. Annie sent a basket, and I can't eat it all meself. It should do for the lot of us."

"Who is 'us'?" Bastian asked again, staring at her with a pan in one hand and a small package of bacon in the other. "And what are you doing here?"

"Didn't Garrett tell ye?" Bette asked quizzically, hoisting her basket onto the dining table. "We're off to roust those bloody remnant from yer castle in the woods, and make it nice and safe, like."

Bastian breathed out a slow breath, trying to dampen the excitement that uncurled in his gut. "You can't, not for me. It's too dangerous and—"

"Those bastards attacked Lord George," Bette reminded him. She pulled out some cloth-wrapped packages and set them on the table. "They're loose in the forest, and it's not safe for travelers."

"How do you know they're the same ones?" Bastian asked, finally putting away the breakfast he had pulled out and grabbing some plates instead. He set them on the table, lifting an eyebrow when Bette gestured for one more plate.

"They're all the bloody same, the beasts," Garrett mumbled as he threw Bastian a bread roll. Bastian caught it and set it down on his plate.

"We don't know, but either way, remnant are there in the castle, and it's too bloody close to the major road. We can't be lettin' them run around like they own the place, can we?"

She eased herself into a chair, absentmindedly rubbing at her now-healed shoulder. Her gesture made Bastian reach for his own again, the last tattered ribbons of his dream brushing against his mind.

Bette frowned, but didn't say anything. Another sharp knock made Bastian forget it altogether.

"Who is it now?" he asked, not expecting an answer. When he pulled open the door, Francis met him with a timid smile.

"Good morning, Bastian. I hope we're not too early?" Francis held out a plate with a fat lump of ham on it.

"Some warning would have been nice," Bastian admitted. "But I won't say no to a slice of that."

"You didn't know?" Francis asked as he came in. "Garrett, you said he invited us!"

"I didn't say it, exactly," Garrett said, words muffled through a mouthful of bread. "I just let ya think I did."

"Oh, ye prick." Bette swatted him on the shoulder. "Poor Bastian, were ye even out of bed?"

Bastian shook his head, reaching for the slab of butter. "Still dreaming. Scared the shit out of me when this idiot came pounding on the door. I thought we'd been attacked."

"We were!" Garrett protested. "A few days ago, anyway."

"Ye wee shite. Pass me that ham." Bette held her knife out. "And slice it for me, too."

"Oh, aye, yer highness." Garrett sliced a thick chunk of ham for Bette and another for himself. "Treatin' me like yer bloody slave."

"As if ye'd change it," Bette scoffed.

Garrett shrugged. "Ye know I wouldn't, but that's no reason ta take so much bloody joy in bossin' me around!"

"As fun as this is," Francis said, "if you're planning to ride out in an hour, we should discuss the plan."

"An hour?" Bastian yelped.

"Aye. Did ye think we'd give 'em time to scare anyone else?" Garrett asked. "I've got me men assemblin' now."

"How many are you taking?" Francis asked. "And who will be left on guard?"

"I'm staying back," Bette said. "Mathias is bein' a shit about it and says I'm not ta go exerting meself fer another day yet."

"I've got Sharne, Jakob, Mathias, and Mack," Garrett said. "Though I'll wager it'll be a one-way trip fer young Jakob. Fair itchin' to see his lass, he is."

"I *hope* he's not itchin'," Bette pointed out. "Or she might catch it off him."

Bastian choked on a bite of food, coughing and spluttering until Garrett gently suggested it was Adeline that gave him the itch in the first place.

Red-faced and unable to breathe, Bastian's chest trembled in a silent laughter as Francis thumped him on the back.

"I would suggest you don't mention that to Jakob," Francis said calmly. Bastian caught the shadow of a suppressed smile tugging at his lips.

"Aye, fair enough," Garrett agreed. "But on to our plan. We'll get Mathias ta scout the area, then we'll run in and thump their heads."

"That's not a plan!" Bette exclaimed.

"It is, too!" Garrett protested.

"Thump their heads is not a plan. Ye need more than that! What if there's a whole horde of them? Or you can't find them? Or," she dropped her voice, eyes wide. "What if they're really a band of monsters disguised as remnant!"

"Stop yer bloody rot, woman, ye'll have the town talkin' of monsters and remnant and hiding in their beds all bloody day!"

"He's got a point," Francis said. "People are already afraid right now. We don't want to be spreading any more rumors."

"Bloody fools," Bette muttered under her breath. "But not as fool as a man without a plan."

"We'll make one up when we get there," Garrett promised. "If there are too many for us to fight, we'll come home and grab a few more bodies."

"And the horses?" Bette asked.

Garrett opened his mouth, closed it, then opened it again. "I know! We'll get Mathias ta ask them ta wait somewhere!"

Bette shook her head. "Ye just thought of that, didn't ye?"

"Aye!" Garrett said, proudly.

Bette shook her head. "Some days I wonder what goes on in yer wee head."

Garrett winked. "I bet ye can guess."

"I don't want to know," Bastian broke in. "Garrett, can I come?"

"Where?" Garrett asked, startled. "To fight the remnant?"

Bastian nodded. "I'll stay out of the way, I swear."

Garrett shot Bette a glance, and she shrugged. "Lad has ta go out there one day. Best let him face the nasty buggers now."

"Alright, then," Garrett said. "But see if ye can convince yer girlfriend ta come, too."

"She's not my girlfriend!" Bastian yelped. "Why do people keep saying that?"

Bette winked. "Ye'll find out sooner 'r later."

Bastian dropped his head, focusing on the food on his plate. Somehow, his appetite had been replaced by the gnawing rumble of nerves. "I should get dressed, then?" he said tentatively, still half-expecting Garrett to tell him to stay home.

"Aye. Get yer ass into some clothes, and meet us at the gates." Garrett took a large bite out of a blueberry muffin, spilling crumbs down his shirt. The rearick rolled his eyes as Bette fussed, trying to brush them off. "Yer just puttin' them in me lap, lass. Leave it—I'll shake off when I stand up."

"Not on my floor, you don't!" Bastian called down.

He quickly undressed, pulling on some sturdy leather pants and a linen shirt. He slipped a stiff leather tunic over it, the only armor he owned. As he laced up the sides, pulling it firmly together, his fingers trembled.

He didn't relish the thought of seeing another remnant. When he had decided not to return to the Temple with Julianne, a wash of relief had soaked him through when he had realized that would mean no journey back through the Madlands. Now, it seemed, the remnant had moved into his territory.

Beneath his fear, he couldn't help but feel grateful towards Bette and Garrett. Despite their claims, there was no real reason to drag a troop of fighters that deep into the woods. He knew they were doing it for him and for his school.

"Not that Garrett isn't a prick," he mumbled, grinning.

Once he had added thick socks and sturdy boots to his attire, Bastian danced downstairs. Garrett was still eating, while Bette stretched back in her seat, watching him. "Yer like a starving pig," she remarked as he shoveled another whole muffin into his mouth.

Garrett tried to reply, but a crumb caught in this throat. His face turned purple, and his eyes watered as he swallowed, an overstated action that made the rearick wince. Heaving a breath that ended in a flurry of coughing, Garrett waved to Bastian.

"I'll be... down... in bit..." the rearick spluttered, before laughing into another hacking cough.

"I'll see you there." Bastian grinned, and darted out the door.

He made his way to the hall, where people were already up and beginning to move about. Jakob and Mathias were outside, saddling horses. A large pack sat next to Jakob's horse.

"Morning," Bastian called. "Have you guys seen Tansy?"

"Inside," Jakob said.

"You'd better be bringing her along," Mathias called after Bastain. "Or she'll have your balls!"

Bastian shook his head, then tiptoed through a few sleeping members of Madam Seher's troop. One end of the hall was set up with tables and behind one, standing with a hand on an out-thrust hip and sporting a pair of fluffy ears, Tansy stood.

Bastian crept past the snoring bodies.

"And he didn't even *tell* me," Tansy said to Madam Seher, her back to Bastian.

Seher's eyes glittered, but didn't leave Tansy's face. "Perhaps he had good reason," she suggested gently.

"Good reason? The man couldn't fight off a swamp rat. I saved his life! And now, he's off hunting remnant while I sit around waiting for him," Tansy snapped.

"You're not exactly sitting around," Bastian said over her shoulder.

Tansy spun around, whipping out a knife that hovered a finger's width away from Bastian's eyeball. When she recognized him, she gave the knife a casual flip and it disappeared.

"And what do you want?" she asked in a lofty voice.

"Well," Bastian said patiently. "A couple of rearick woke me up this morning. Apparently, they're leading a raid on the remnant we found at the ruins."

Tansy narrowed her eyes suspiciously. "You only found out this morning?"

Bastian nodded. "Though, everyone else seems to believe Garrett told me first. I asked if I could come, and he said yes."

"He said you could go?" Her nostrils flared.

"Yes," Bastian said. "And where I go, you go, right?"

She regarded him, pouting, then nodded once.

"So? Are you going to get ready or what?"

Flashing a grin, Tansy threw her arms around Bastian's neck. "I never doubted you for a second!" she cried, despite all evidence to the contrary. She dashed over to a small pile of neatly stacked belongings in one corner of the hall.

A few minutes later she was ready, an ornate leather corset and matching leg guards strapped on, and weapons dropped into every pocket or strap she could reach.

She spun to face Bastian when she was done. "Are you still standing there?" she asked. "Hurry up! We'll be late!"

She danced off out of the hall, leaving Bastian to follow behind. The gates of Tahn were already open for the morning and a group clustered around them, listening to Garrett shout instructions.

"And we're not going to engage the bastards if there's too many!" he yelled, scowling. "Ye hear?"

"Define 'too many', Sarge," Sharne said dryly.

Garrett's eyes twinkled. "About as many as would cause us certain death... plus ten."

The team in front of Garrett saluted, then turned back to their horses.

"Took yer sweet ass time, mystic," Garrett grumbled. "Hope ye weren't suckin' face behind a barn somewhere."

Bastian gulped, but as an apology to Tansy reached his lips, the girl beside him scoffed.

"You just wish it was you, rearick," she said with a laugh. "Now, stop teasing. If Bastian's face gets any redder, it'll start to glow—and we don't want a shining beacon to warn the remnant we're coming, now, do we?"

"Aye, that's a fair point," Garrett said with a wide grin. "Now, get yer horses and let's go!" He waved his hand, gesturing at two small mares that were saddled and ready.

Tansy vaulted onto hers in a single jump. Bastian sighed, and clumsily clambered onto his. No matter the days he had spent in the saddle since leaving the temple, he always felt gangly and awkward on horseback.

"Ride out!" Garrett called.

He led the way, Mathias and Jakob riding abreast behind him. Sharne and Mack rode next, and Tansy and Bastian brought up the rear.

"He really thinks we can handle that many remnant?" Bastian asked, nerves digging into his gut.

Tansy shrugged. "If we kill three each, that's twenty-one dead —though, I'd wager Garrett alone could take down five, at least, and the physical mage could kill even more than that."

Bastian snorted. "You think I could take down a remnant? On my own?"

Tansy lifted her head. "You won't be alone, mystic. Stay by me, and I'll make sure you come home in one piece."

Once clear of the town, the horses launched into a trot, then settled into a canter. The trees passed by in a flash, and all too soon, the forest loomed overhead.

"There it is!" Garrett called, pointing at the snarled, burnt metal pole. He reigned in his horse and ambled up, muttering, "The bastards."

"What is it?" Bastian called, picking his way through the others.

The Iron Tree had been smooth and pale when he had seen it last. Now, it was black, painted with some kind of flaking, crusted substance. Bastian reached out and pressed a finger to the tacky surface.

"Blood," Garrett said.

Bastian snatched his hand back and wiped it on his shirt, forcing down a sudden nausea.

"A warning?" Sharne asked.

"Aye." Garrett looked up, eyes shining over a wide smile. "They don't know what's comin' fer 'em."

He casually turned his horse down the path to the ruins, and they followed single-file down the narrow trail.

Bastian kept his eyes up, darting from tree to tree and from trees to ground. He flicked his eyes ahead to Tansy and saw her hands resting lightly on two short swords.

"How are you doing that?" he called in a low voice.

"Doing what?" she asked, twisting to look back at him.

"You're riding with no hands. Hell, now you're doing it backwards!"

She grimaced. "It's all in the knees. Though, it would be easier with no saddle."

She turned back, leaving Bastian to shake his head in wonder. The girl seemed to be capable of anything.

They reached the ruins, and Bastian sniffed, then blanched. "I smell blood," he said.

"Aye," Garrett grumbled. "Looks like they left us a wee gift."

In the middle of the ruins a group of animal bones was piled up, clumps of fur and tendons still attached. Flies buzzed noisily, and Bastian swatted one away, clenching his teeth to keep his breakfast down.

"The horses should wait back at the Iron Tree," Mathias said. "They are feeling afraid. I don't know that I'll be able to calm them enough to make them useful."

Garrett dismounted. "Very well. Send them off. We can't fight with them in the forest, anyway. Sharne, Jakob, scout the immediate area. Mack, ye can go with Sharne. She'll keep ye out of trouble."

The two fighters slipped down from their horses and darted into the trees without a sound.

"Ye see anythin'?" Garrett asked Mathias.

The druid stopped fiddling with the strap on one of the horses, and his eyes lit up, shining green in the dim morning light.

"Nothing nearby," he said. "Let me send Percival a little farther out."

The druid paused. Then, he sucked in a sharp breath. "Looks like we might have gotten more than we bargained for, rearick."

"What is it?" Garrett asked urgently.

"There's a horde of them. I see them clustered across the river. A fire—no, two. Rubbish, a dead boar. Garrett, I think I can see buildings. They've set up a permanent group." The horse danced back. Mathias's eyes cleared, and he shook his head, reaching out to sooth the beast.

"Bullshit," Garrett spat. "Remnant don't group, not like that. They're roaming hordes. Like ants!"

"Ants have colonies," Mathias said.

"Ach, like fucking bears then."

"They don't roam. Garrett, have you ever *seen* a bear?" Mathias asked, unable to keep his face straight.

"Are you *laughing* at me, ye donkey's dick?" Garrett snapped, hands on his hips.

"Me? Laughing? Not at all." Mathias's lips twitched again, and he casually rubbed his mouth to hide it.

"Ahh, go fuck yerself. They're across the river, ye say?"

Mathias nodded. "We'll be able to see them, but I wouldn't advise getting too close."

"Right, then." Garrett hooked his thumbs in his belt and

leaned back. "We'll go take a peek and see what the bastards are up to, then decide if we need more men."

"Garrett, we need more men," Mathias said flatly.

Tansy shot a worried glance at Bastian. He gave her a brave grin, despite his worry.

"Aye," the rearick said. "But we'll need to know how many, and if we can bring in equipment to help."

Mathias bowed his head. "Very well. But I'm serious, rearick—there's a lot of them. I've never seen anything like it, even in the Madlands."

Garrett chewed his whiskers, the first sign that his confidence was waning. Still, he didn't change his orders.

Jakob, Mack, and Sharne returned. "No sign of anything nasty in the trees," Sharne assured him.

Garrett nodded. "The moldy pricks are across the river," Garrett said. "We'll go to the bank, see if we can't find out what they're up to."

"You think they're a risk, Sarge?" Sharne asked. "Because you sound like you did that time you had to tell Bette you got drunk and threw up in her helmet."

"It wasn't the drink!" Garrett protested. "It was me dinner, and that's that!"

"Sure, Sarge," she said, rolling her eyes. "But you were still shaking in your boots when she found out, and you had that exact look on your face, too." She thrust a finger at him.

"Shut yer face, woman," Garrett grumbled. "We're just bein' careful, is all. The ant-speaker here says there might be a few more than we thought."

"Plus ten?" Mack asked with a grin.

"Aye," Garrett said, face serious.

Mack raised an eyebrow.

"Come on, then," Sharne said. "The sooner we find out what they're up to, the sooner we can put a stop to it."

Garrett led the way, Mathias by his side to point out trails and paths the animals used to travel the forest. Sharne dropped back to speak with Bastian and Tansy.

"Can you see what he's thinking, mystic?" she asked.

"I could," Bastian said, "but I'd get my balls cut off if he found out."

"We wouldn't want that!" Tansy said, miming a look of horror.

Bastian regarded her suspiciously. "I can't tell how sarcastic you're being," he said.

She laughed. "I've never told you lot to stay out of my head."

"No," Bastian said, "but you're shielded. I mean, I could break through that, but that's not socially acceptable. Or polite."

Tansy raised an eyebrow, so Bastian gently sent a tendril of mental magic her way, expecting to be met with a fairly strong shield. To his surprise, there was nothing. He slipped into her mind to see what she was thinking.

As fast as he was in, he shot out again, an image of himself burned into his mind. He had been down at the river behind Tahn, bathing after helping to butcher a deer. Tansy must have followed and spotted him. She had helped that day, so it wouldn't have been unreasonable. The brief flash of memory showed him stretching, his pale, slender figure glistening in the sunlight.

"You're such a perve!" Bastian gasped. "What the hell, Tansy?"

She burst into laughter, quickly hushed by Garrett. "It was an accident, I didn't know you had already gone down there. Don't get your knickers in a twist. It's not like I stripped off and joined you."

Bastian clamped his mouth shut, refusing to rise to her bait, even as his cheeks burned. She clutched her stomach with one hand, the other clamped over her mouth to stifle her laughter.

"Settle down, you two," Sharne said, though she, too, was smiling. "You don't want to bring down a remnant raiding party on our heads.

Tansy sobered immediately. "What exactly are we walking into?" she asked.

Sharne sighed. "Hopefully? Nothing. We sneak in, get an idea of their numbers, and run like hell. If it's as bad as I think, we don't want to catch their attention."

"And if we do?" Bastian asked, anxiety rising again as his mind brushed over the very real possibility of this coming to a fight they couldn't win.

Sharne shrugged. "We fight. We hope help comes." She regarded him carefully. "If they see you're afraid, they'll come for you first," she said. "Stay back. Stay low. Don't stick your neck out if you can help it."

"We'll keep you safe, love," Tansy said. For once, there wasn't a hint of sarcasm in her words.

Bastian blew out a slow breath as, up ahead, Garrett called for the party to halt.

CHAPTER TWENTY-FIVE

"There's the river," Garrett called softly. "We go south."

They stayed behind the trees as they followed the river down-stream. Over the gurgling water, Bastian heard the clink of stone on metal. He held up a hand, and the whole party stopped.

"What's that?" he asked in a loud whisper, cupping one ear.

Garrett gestured for Bastian to come up beside him. He pointed across the water. "See that?" he asked.

Through the smatter of leaves and over the spray of water on rocks, Bastian saw it. A remnant, sitting on the other side of the water, whacking at a furred body with a rusted knife.

The remnant stopped, laying the knife down to push its hand inside the corpse. It pulled out and lifted a small organ. Blood ran down its arm as he lifted it to his nose, then licked it.

"That's revolting," Bastian whispered under his breath.

"Look beyond." Garrett gently nudged Bastian to one side. As he moved, leaning his head to look round a fat tree trunk, Bastian's heart dropped into his boots.

A flat clearing dotted with stubby buildings lay beyond. At least twelve remnant were visible, sitting by their kills or stuffing meat into their mouths. A fire pit smoked in the middle.

"Oh, shit," Bastian whimpered.

"A shit on the ground is a wee inconvenience," Garrett told him. "This? This is a Bitch-damned clusterfuck."

They withdrew back into the trees.

"So, what now?" Jakob asked. "Do we risk engaging them?"

Garrett bit down hard on a clump of beard, letting it tug at his skin as he chewed it. "I think me lass would skin me alive if we did."

"I can send for reinforcements," Mathias said. "It will be faster than travelling back ourselves. We don't want to let the opportunity go to waste, do we?"

Garrett's eyes shot open wide, and he grinned. "Perfect! Then if we… err, accidentally start a tousle, she can't say I broke me promise!"

"Wait," Bastian said. "You mean you'd run on in there, sword raised, if you weren't scared of Bette?"

Garrett looked shocked. "I'm no' scared of her. I just know how to keep me hide in one piece, is all."

Mathias cupped his hands, and he whistled into them, a trilling bird call that echoed through the forest sounding just like a normal animal call. A moment later, a bird noisily flapped down from the canopy.

"Here, Percival," Mathias said, pulling a tiny pen from his belt. A thin ribbon of parchment wrapped around its shaft, and he unfurled a length, tearing it off. "Take this to Bette. No, that's Tessa—Yes, I *know* she feeds you, but this isn't about your lunch. *Bette!*"

Once the note was secured, the bird jumped off his hand with a rough flutter of wings. Mathias watched it weave between the trees, almost smacking into one, then veering off to one side before correcting its course.

"I don't know what I did to deserve such an idiot familiar," he muttered. "If he wasn't so loyal, he'd be dinner."

At Bastian's horrified look, Mathias shrugged. "It was a joke. More or less."

A warbling yell came from the other side of the river, and Garrett peeked out through the trees again. "Would ye look at that!" he exclaimed.

Bastian nudged Mathias aside to join the rearick. Across the water, by the cooking fire, a band of five remnant had gathered. One stood apart, noticeable for his layers and layers of brightly colored clothing scraps.

He wore a battered helmet, one side smeared with some kind of dark paint. *Probably blood*, Bastian thought with distaste.

The remnant leader jumped onto a rock. "We hunt?" he called, and the others raised a cry in agreement.

"We hunt!" they chanted. "Hunt with Chet!"

Chet yelled over them, crying, "We hunt big meal today! We eat and be strong and kill monster if they come!"

"Chet! Chet! Chet!" The rallying cry made Bastian shiver.

"That is *not* normal behavior for a remnant," he whispered to Garrett.

"No," Garrett said, watching two of the hunters jostle each other. Then, one turned and stabbed the other in the throat with a knife. "But that is. Wonder what could have brought them together like that?"

"Whatever it is, it's bad news for us," Jakob said. "An organized enemy is always harder than one with no bonds."

"They're remnant, lad," Garrett said confidently. "They might call one name today, but if there's a fresh feed in it, they'll stab his guts and sit on the body while they eat it."

Jakob frowned, unconvinced. He watched the band of hunters run across the river, slipping on stones and splashing the shallow water as they went. "Looks like they're headed south of us, but we should pull back."

Garrett hesitated, then nodded. "Aye." He let the leaves fall back over the scene ahead and nodded to Jakob. "We'll go back to the ruins. Once we've a few more bodies with us, we'll go clean the bastards out."

"Do you want eyes on their camp or the hunting party?" Mathias asked, his eyes green.

"Watch the camp," Garrett said. "We know there were six of them with old Chet or Shit or whatever he calls himself. I want to know how many are back there."

The druid nodded, and his brows drew together as he concentrated, keeping half an eye on the path ahead while he used his animal-sight to watch the remnant camp.

"Do you think waiting at the ruins is wise?" Bastian asked, hurrying up to walk beside Garrett. "That's where they attacked us last time."

Garrett shook his head. "They won't return there, not after the thrashin' yer lass gave them."

The mention of Tansy made Bastian's ears burn. He glanced back at her. She walked by Jakob's side, chatting about something as she skipped along, unimpeded by the heavy forest growth.

"So ye do have yer eye on 'er," Garrett said, grinning.

"What?" Bastian yelped. "I didn't say that!"

"No, but yer face did!" Garrett barked, slapping his thigh. "Ah, ye poor, naïve, wee thing. That girl has ye wrapped around 'er finger, and ye don't even know it yet, do ye?"

"I'm not wrapped around her anything," Bastian grumbled. He couldn't help another glance back, though. His eyes met Tansy's, and she winked at him, sending his emotions scattering to every end of the spectrum. "Bitch's oath," he muttered.

"Aye, that's about how I felt when young Bette caught me eye," Garrett said knowingly. "I had me head in such a state I didn't know if I liked her, or if I wanted to run away!"

"So, you dueled her instead," Bastain sighed. "It's different for a rearick."

"Aye?" Garrett said. "How's that?"

"You're built for fighting!" Bastian exclaimed, then remembered to lower his voice. "You're tough and brave, and you can kill remnant just by looking at them! I'm weak and pasty and jump at my own damn shadow."

"Ye got brains, though," Garrett said, tapping his head. "Some lasses like a man with a good head. Not so much as a man who gives it, but there's no sayin' ye can't—"

Garrett's words were cut off by a warbling scream behind them. Bastian spun to see three remnant racing up the trail behind them.

"Go!" Garrett yelled. "Get ta the ruins! We can fight 'em there!"

Bastian didn't need to be told twice. He turned and ran—but not before stopping to grab Tansy's hand, pulling her along with him.

She raced along beside him, seemingly without effort. "Why, Bastian," she said, voice jumping as she vaulted over a fallen tree. "Did you just think of my safety before yours?"

"I figured you'll save my ass later," he quipped. "You can't do that if a remnant is wearing you like a winter coat."

"Cheeky bastard," she giggled, then dropped his hand and sprinted ahead to leap through the crumbling wall.

Bastian heaved himself through, then turned to help Sharne and Mathias climb through the gap.

Garrett and Jakob stood at either side, waiting until the others were safe behind the wall.

"Shall we stand here, rearick?" Jakob asked.

Garrett shook his head. "Inside. The boy needs ta get 'is hands bloody, and he can't do that if we kill the bastards out here."

He grinned, and as Jakob levitated himself over the wall, Garrett plunged through the gap himself, rolling to his feet on the other side.

Silence fell. The air was heavy with anticipation as the team stood waiting for the remnant to bust through the narrow space between the stones.

"Do ye think we scared 'em off?" Mack whispered.

"I don't think I'd say they're feeling scared," Tansy said, voice wavering.

Bastian turned to her, taking in her raised arm and wide eyes. On top of the tiny, crumbling room he had seen on his previous visit, a remnant stood, bright scraps of clothing flapping in the breeze.

Chet bared his yellowed teeth in a wicked grin, then vaulted to the ground, barking out a loud, wordless cry. The noise set off a cacophony of yells and hoots as remnant swarmed the walls, slithering over and dropping to the ground even as others poured through the openings on all sides.

"*AMBUSH!*" Garrett hollered, backing up as he drew his sword.

"Stay with me," Tansy snapped to Bastian, moving between him and a remnant.

Bastian's breath stuck in his throat as time slowed. He watched a remnant leap into the air towards them, loose skin slowly contorting as it left the ground, seeming to float before gradually falling to land on one steady foot.

Bastian blinked, and time resumed. Before he could suck a gasp into his starved lungs, the remnant was on them, clawing at Tansy's face before she kicked him away, then spun to plant a dagger in its eye.

The remnant fell, howling and clutching its face. Another one appeared to take its place.

Tansy put a hand behind her, shoving Bastian stumbling back before swinging her knives around. A slice across the remnant's belly spilled intestines on the ground, releasing the smell of shit into the air.

"Either get down, or fight!" Tansy yelled, then jumped into the air, landing on a soft body with one foot and using it as a launch pad to spring into a duo of remnant that had descended on Sharne.

Bastian yanked out his sword, holding it out with a white-knuckled grip. A remnant saw him and grinned before sauntering over with a jagged, broken knife.

Cries of *"Chet, Chet!"* rang out sporadically, and the monster headed for Bastian echoed the chant in a guttural growl.

The remnant flew back and slammed into a wall. Bastian jumped and spun to see what had made him change course. Jakob gave him a quick salute before twisting his hands again and sending a fiery blast into the fallen enemy.

"I'm not cut out for this shit," Bastian gasped as Garrett slid across the ground in front of him, then rolled into an attack stance and slammed his sword up between a remnant's legs.

Warm drops sprayed on Bastian's face, and he wiped his eyes with a sleeve, swallowing hard when he saw the smear of blood on his shirt.

Eyes darting back to Tansy, Bastian saw her facing off with two remnant, expertly darting her weapons back and forth to block their blows, landing small cuts on them every few seconds. Both dripped with blood, but gave no sign they noticed the wounds.

Behind her, a remnant wrestled with Mack, until the soldier shoved the beast away and was immediately body slammed by another one. The freed remnant spotted Tansy and hissed.

It ran for her, and Bastian realized she had no chance of disengaging her attackers to face the new threat. His heart lurched as he threw himself forwards, running on light feet to slam his shoulder into the remnant.

They flew sideways, and the creature landed in the dirt. Bastian managed to keep his footing, but only just. As his foe scampered back and jumped to its feet, Bastian softened his knees and dropped into the stance Bette had taught him.

"Now or never," the mystic muttered, as his death grinned back.

CHAPTER TWENTY-SIX

Marcus staggered at the top of the mountain and collapsed to his knees. Julianne still lay in his arms, limp and unmoving. Sweat dripped down his back, chilling his skin to send wracking shivers down his spine when he stopped.

Julianne groaned and twitched. "Leave me alone," she muttered.

"Jules?" Marcus shook her gently, careful not to jar her sore arm.

Her eyes flashed open and filled with white, her face still. Then, she wriggled away from him, sitting flat on the snow-covered ground.

"Help!" he called weakly.

"Donna's here," she said urgently. "Inside. But they think she's—"

The old, oaken doors to the temple groaned and swung open.

"Master?" a white-robed man ran out, ignoring Marcus as he knelt by Julianne, heedless of the snow on his knees. "Master, why are you out in this weather?"

"We weren't exactly given a warm welcome in Craigston," Marcus explained. "Or we would have stayed there."

"William," Julianne snapped, pulling herself up on Marcus's arm. "Where is Aldred? I need to see him, now."

She let go of Marcus, straightened, and took a few steps before stumbling. He caught her, and she gave him a grateful smile. "William?" she prodded.

The gaping guard jumped, and his eyes flashed white. "He's coming, Master." William's lips parted as if he wanted to speak. Then, he paused, darting a glance around before closing them again.

"Something you need to say, William?" Marcus asked. His place here was uncertain—he wasn't a mystic and had no title of his own—but his need to protect Julianne overrode that.

"No," Julianne said before the guard could speak. "Everything is fine. William, could you make sure a meal is set out for me in the dining room?"

William frowned, but nodded and went inside, leaving Marcus and Julianne to follow slowly.

"What's going on?" Marcus asked. "I wasn't sure I'd be able to wake you up when we got here."

"I... had some help," Julianne said cryptically. "I'm not functioning as well as I should be, but I'll be ok. I won't be able to use magic for a while though—it's all I can do to keep my shields intact."

"Duly noted." Marcus let go of her to shove the door back open, so she could pass.

As she did, she whispered, "Don't trust *anyone* here. Not everything is as it seems."

Marcus's eyes widened, but he didn't answer, seeing another robed mystic hurrying along towards them.

"Master," the greying man said stiffly. "Who is this?"

"A friend," Julianne said. "Aldred is my master of the guard," she explained to Marcus.

"We've just returned from our journey," Marcus said. "And your Master needs a meal, and medical attention."

Aldred's eyes shot wide. "You just…"

"Hush, Aldred," Julianne said. "Marcus, please, don't let on we're just back. They think I've been here for two solid weeks."

Aldred swallowed, face pale. Marcus cursed, but Julianne smiled. "It's fine. He didn't try to kill us on the spot, so I'm assuming Aldred is safe to speak to."

Aldred stammered an apology, then stopped, scowling. Finally, he spat, "What the *fuck* is going on? Who are you?"

Julianne sighed tiredly. "I'm me, Aldred. And yes, I just returned. We defeated the New Dawn, but Donna slipped away— I think the magic she was exposed to has warped her mind a little."

"You mean—" Aldred stopped, then dropped into a whisper. "You mean, *she's Donna?*"

"Who?" Marcus asked, shaking his head with confusion.

Aldred glared his way silently, and Marcus bristled at the suspicion on his face.

"The other me," Julianne said flatly.

"So, you know about that," Aldred said. "Master, if it's really you… please, I don't want to have to force through. Your shields."

"Just for a moment," she warned. "I don't know what that psychopath is up to, and I'm in no state to defend against her, not yet."

Marcus watched as both Julianne's and Aldred's eyes flashed white. Julianne's faded quickly, while Aldred's continued to glow. A moment later, Marcus felt a gentle pressure on his mind.

Strengthening his shield, Marcus grinned. "Sorry, friend. Julianne might trust you, but I don't know you—and right now, I wouldn't trust my own mother if she was standing next to you."

Marcus didn't mention that his mother was dead these last seven years—if she had been there, he would reach for a knife before a hug.

Aldred sighed. "Fair enough." He bowed to Julianne, a deep, reverent gesture. "You have my deepest apologies, Master. We have suspected the one with your face is not who she seems, but the authority of the position…"

"Turns you into a horde of dithering idiots," Julianne finished for him. "I'm a leader, not a precocious god."

A smile touched Aldred's lips. "Ah, yes. It's definitely you."

Julianne swallowed, and Marcus winced at the dark circles beneath her eyes. "Aldred, your Master really does need help."

Aldred jumped and nodded. "I'll send for someone. Perhaps… Oh, Bitch help me. You wouldn't know…"

"That Margit is dead?" Julianne asked. "It's ok. I found out earlier. Terribly sad."

Marcus's breath caught, and pain sank into his chest. Julianne had spoken of Margit like a favorite grandmother, someone she loved and trusted above all others. She had often joked that if he didn't meet Margit's approval, their relationship would just have to end.

Where the hell did she hear that? Marcus wondered.

Her face gave no hint of the grief she must be feeling, but he tried to believe that it was because she really was strong enough to handle the news. Still, she didn't look strong… she looked downright nonchalant.

Marcus's lips pressed together while his brain raced over the possibilities. All he knew was there was something she wasn't telling him—and as they entered the Temple dining hall, this wasn't the time or the place to ask what.

He had promised to trust her, so that's all he could do. When it was safe, she would tell him what the hell was going on.

Julianne slowly walked past the few mystics dining in the cavernous hall. Marcus watched as eyes slid their way, quickly appraising the newcomer before quickly averting. The low hum of conversation quickly fell under a stifling blanket of silence.

Three of the diners walked out, and Marcus saw one still held a plate full of barely-touched food.

"Donna must have really done a number on these guys,"

Marcus said. "That, or your stories about the level of fun in this place were way overstated."

"Hey," Julianne chided quietly. "We're fun. Most of the time."

"You must be right." Marcus looked around, taking in the somber faces as Julianne slid into a seat a little larger than the others at the head of the table. He took the seat next to hers. "I can't imagine Danil coming from a place like *this*."

Julianne snorted. "I don't know *where* Danil came from. He says he was born on a farm, but I swear, the man was raised in a bawdy tavern. Or maybe a brothel…"

"For all his talk, I don't think he's ever stepped foot near a prostitute before he met Polly," Marcus said, grinning.

He noticed a few curious looks turning their way, and he blinked as his shield wobbled under the pressure of several mental probes. He slowed his breathing and locked his eyes on Julianne's.

"You good?" she asked softly.

He gave the slightest nod, then jumped as a young woman trotted up to them with a platter of warm bread and sliced fruit, and a pitcher of elixir with a glass. "Master, I'm so sorry. We just got William's message." She deposited the tray and waited, posture tight and lips in a tight line.

"That's fine, Daisy," Julianne said. "Tell the cook I said thank you, and sorry to put her to such a bother outside of meal time."

A look of confusion flitted across Daisy's face as she dropped a quick curtsy. Once she had scurried away, Marcus leaned close to Julianne.

"Are young girls normally that terrified of you here?" he asked.

"Not if they behave," Julianne said wryly. "I think that 'other me' has been a bit short on manners, though, and they're already used to her abrupt orders." Then, she groaned. "Oh, Bastard's luck."

Marcus looked up to see a middle-aged man headed their

way, carrying a small basket. His face was drawn, and his eyes cast to the floor.

"Jonsen!" Julianne's voice was laced with false cheer. "I see you're finally living your dream."

Jonsen looked up warily. "I beg your pardon?"

Julianne dropped her voice, looking him directly in the eyes. "I remember you once told me that when your magic manifested, you were disappointed it wasn't nature-based. You said you'd always wanted to be a druid."

Jonsen's face trembled, and he frowned, burying his attention in the small pile of bandages he had brought.

"And now, here you are, patching me up," Julianne said, more loudly.

Jonsen carefully lifted Julianne's arm. He probed it carefully, and she sucked in a hissing breath, jaw dimpling as she clenched her teeth.

"You ok, Jules?" Marcus asked.

"Fine." Her voice was strained.

"I'm afraid you have a break, or at least a fracture." Jonsen sighed. "We will have to send to Arcadia for help. I'm not even sure the rearick would be able to help in their med hall. I'm afraid my meagre talent isn't enough to treat this, apart from basic care."

He helped Julianne to wrap the arm in a piece of fabric, strapping it down to her chest to keep it still.

"There," he said, patting it hard enough to make her wince. "All done."

"Thank the Bitch for that," Julianne muttered. "Sorry, Jonsen, I care for you dearly, but you're about as gentle as a shit-faced moose."

Jonsen sucked in a small, fast gasp, his eyes widening. Instead of the shock or irritation Marcus had expected, the man's eyes filled as his mouth parted in desperate hope.

"Master?" he whispered quietly. "You're... *you* again?"

"Damn straight," she said. "Don't say anything, though. I'm not sure what we're dealing with yet."

Jonsen nodded, a sharp, jerky motion. Then, he quickly piled up the bandages and hurried away.

"I've lost my appetite," Julianne said. She reached for the elixir and downed it in a long swallow. "Oh, my dear elixir. I've missed you so much."

Marcus raised an eyebrow as she held the cup to her chest. She grinned at him.

"I love you too, Marcus, but until you've gone from drinking the nectar of the gods on a daily basis to sipping under-aged wine, you can't know how glad I am to be back."

"We'd best get you to bed," he said. "Because you may not have noticed the herbs floating in that pitcher, but I did."

"Herbs?" Julianne stood, leaning over the table to peer in. "Well, whaddya know?" Her cheeks flushed as her smile widened. "My thanks to the chef."

Marcus chuckled. "Fast acting, I see."

Julianne nodded, then frowned. "I shouldn't have drunk that. I need to be on my guard. I can't fight Donna if I'm wiped out on sedatives."

Marcus shot out of his seat, alarmed. "What about your shield?" He hissed quietly. "Are you in danger? I'll carry you back down that damned mountain if I have to."

"Don't be silly," Julianne said. She gripped the table with one hand to steady herself and her eyes turned white, the soft, familiar glow a comfort to Marcus. They cleared. "There. I can focus past it now."

"Wait," Marcus said, catching her free arm as she turned away from the table. "You just… magicked away the effects of a drug?"

Julianne snorted. "Nope. But I did make sure I'll stay awake. You've never been drunk and had to turn up for guard duty?" she asked, making her way to the door.

Marcus nodded, eyes quickly taking in the plush tapestries

they passed and memorizing the route they took through the winding Temple hallways. "And no, I won't tell you how drunk, or how often."

She giggled. "You were still drunk, but you concentrated hard enough that no one noticed, right?"

Marcus nodded. That wasn't entirely right—old Dickerson had caught on, more than once—but he had gotten away with it a few times.

Julianne shrugged. "It's like that. I still can't walk in a straight line, and I'm tired as hell, but I refuse to notice." That may have been true, but Marcus waited as Julianne glared at a stairwell, as if trying to flatten it with her mental powers. Finally, she steeled herself and started up them.

"Damn," Marcus remarked. "I could have used that trick back in my soldiering days."

Julianne clicked her tongue disapprovingly. "You don't mean to tell me the good citizens of Arcadia have had to rely on a drunk guardsman, do you?"

Marcus chuckled. "I never pretended to be an angel. Some of the stories I could tell would curl your toes."

Julianne paused at the top of the steps, rubbing her face.

"You really should go for a lie down, Jules," Marcus said gently. He hoped his insistence wouldn't make her fight the idea harder.

To his surprise, she nodded. "That's where I'm going now." She gestured ahead. "My rooms are down at the end, and my beautiful, wonderful bed is in there. I plan to have a very intimate reunion with it in about twelve seconds."

"Unlike you to actually take a break when you need one," Marcus pointed out. "Not that I'm saying it's a bad thing."

"I know when I'm bordering on useless," she answered. "Bitch's oath, Marcus. I'm tired, sore, and my head is absolutely pounding. I need meditation and sleep—and not necessarily in that order."

Feet pounded up the stairs behind them, and Aldred emerged into the stairway.

"Master Julianne," he panted. "News from Craigston. It's the rearick—they're marching against us!"

"They're what?" Marcus snapped. "What do you mean *against* us?"

Aldred shot him a look, but Julianne nodded for the master guardsman to explain. "They sent a messenger ahead. A rearick soldier came, he said if we don't hand you over, they'll attack the Temple!"

Aldred's voice shook, rising higher with every word until it finally broke on the last.

Julianne sighed. "How far are they?"

"I sent scouts straight out. They estimate we have about two hours," Aldred said.

"Well, then," Julianne said. "At least I have time for a nap before they get here."

"A nap?" Aldred said, voice no more than a whimper.

Julianne sighed. "I literally can't think past the end of my nose. If I don't rest, I'll fall down."

Aldred took in Julianne's pale face and the dark circles under her eyes. He gave a curt nod, then turned to Marcus. "You're a soldier?" he asked.

"Yes," Marcus replied, straightening. "I served Arcadia, fought in the rebellion, and served Arcadia again afterwards. I led the battle for Tahn alongside Julianne and helped to free Muir from the New Dawn, too."

Aldred frowned at the unfamiliar place names, but turned to Julianne. "Master, what we are facing... it's beyond my experience."

Julianne touched his shoulder. "It's beyond all of us, Aldred. Rearick marching against the mystics? Never in all of history have we faced such a trial." Her hand fell away, and she straightened. "Marcus will assist you. Trust his advice. He's wiser than he looks."

Marcus rolled his eyes at that.

"I'll send William up to stand at your door." Aldred's eyes glowed as he sent the mental message. "Master, if I may—your shield? It's shutting off my ability to speak with you."

"I can't drop it," she explained. "Or I may never get it back up again. I don't know where Donna is or what she's up to, but I can't risk letting her in my head."

Aldred nodded. "Of course, Master Julianne."

Julianne leaned in to hug Marcus, whispering in his ear as she relaxed into him. "Help them prepare for the worst, my love… but *do not* let this come to war." She pushed back and stepped away. "Come and fetch me before they arrive," she said.

Heavy boots clomped at the stairs and William appeared. He jogged over to them.

"Your job is to keep Master Julianne safe," Aldred said. "At all costs."

William nodded and stood at attention, his eyes turning white. Aldred shook his head.

"No!" the master guardsman snapped. "Full shield. If we need you, I'll send a man on foot."

William nodded, and Aldred hurried away, Marcus by his side.

Julianne slipped into her room and inhaled deeply. The scent of old lavender still hung gently in the stale air.

"So," said William, hovering in the air. "It's really you?"

Julianne smiled gently. "The one and only." She pulled at the bed spread, awkwardly tugging it down.

William darted in to help her, expertly turning it down before helping her out of her long, white robe. Julianne slid between the clean sheets, basking in the cool, crisp feel after weeks on the road.

"I was beginning to think I'd never see you again, Master Julianne," William said softly.

"You already did," Julianne said. "Outside, in the snow. That was me—the real me."

"Oh, no," William said, laughing. "That wasn't *me*. That was the *real* William."

Julianne lurched upright, but the man towering above her shoved her back. He leaned down, pressing Julianne's injured arm, and tugged a pillow over her face to smother her agonized cry.

The fabric pressed against her mouth, but a rough hand tugged it away from the top of her face to let her see Donna staring down at her.

"Oh, Julianne. I'm *so* glad you're back." Donna gave Julianne's arm another twist. "It's a pity we can't play just now. You see, I have a war to kick off."

Pain lanced through Julianne, and her stomach roiled, as a veil of darkness slowly closed over her. She reached out to the one person she knew could help, but, swamped by agony and muddled by sedatives, her magic crumbled before she finally lost consciousness completely.

CHAPTER TWENTY-SEVEN

Bastian bared his teeth and braced hard as the remnant lunged at him. A clumsy strike saw his sword clatter to the ground. The remnant grabbed a hunk of Bastian's hair and jerked his head forwards, gnashing broken teeth at Bastian's neck.

Bastian shoved, punching the beast's throat until it let go. He stumbled back, and a second body slam threw him to the ground. The remnant growled and spat, screaming obscenities as the mystic desperately shielded his face with one arm, punching and flailing with the other as the remnant pummeled Bastian's head.

A blow to the gut made Bastian's diaphragm spasm, then freeze. His mouth opened like a drowning fish as he tried to suck air back into his chest.

"Weak!" the remnant screamed. "Weak! You no warrior, you weak!"

A boot planted in the dirt by Bastian's head, and through his oxygen-starved mind, he recognized it as Tansy's. A flash of sunlight on metal left spots in his vision.

Bastian stretched out, and the remnant saw its chance. It dove, mouth open, towards Bastian's cheek. Teeth sank in and pain speared his face even as his fingers fumbled for purchase on Tansy's boot.

He found it. Her knife—one of them, anyway—slipped out, clutched in numb fingers as he stabbed. His first strike sank into flesh and the remnant howled, flesh pulling from Bastian's face and breaking away with a sickening twang.

He thrust the knife again, aiming under the chin of the remnant as it was distracted by the flood of blood spurting from its neck. The remnant jerked as the knife smoothly slid through flesh, tendon, and finally brain.

Lungs finally cooperating, Bastian gasped and heaved the dead weight of the remnant off his chest. He rolled to his knees, and retched until a rough hand yanked his shirt from the back, pulling him up.

"Ye pansy," Garrett cried. "Stop pukin' an' start killin'!"

Bastian reeled as Garrett let him go, stumbling two steps to the side before Garrett grabbed him again.

"Fuck's sake, lad. Tomorrow, you'll report fer mornin' trainin'. No excuses!" Garrett paused to run his sword through the guts of a charging remnant. "Bah. Take this an' try not ta get yerself killed." He shoved the dripping sword at Bastian.

"There are too many," Bastian panted, his eyes glowing white as he used his magic to block out the pain in his cheek. "We can't win this."

"Me lassie will be along soon enough," Garrett said, grinning. A horse whinnied loudly and yells of "Tahn!" rang out across the battleground. "There she is now! Go find yer girl and stick by her. She'll keep ye safe."

Garrett stepped on a dead remnant, craning his neck to see over Mack and Sharne, back to back in the center of a ring of remnant. Mack fought with force, chopping and swinging his heavy sword to lop off limbs and, as Garrett watched, a head.

Sharne was lighter, faster. She stabbed and cut, slicing open a throat, then a belly, and taking off the fingertips of a remnant who reached out to claw at her face.

Beyond, a horse galloped out of the greenery, Bette astride the nag's back and yelling orders.

"Seventh stance! Form up! Let's take these bastards down!"

Her eyes scanned the battle, finally netting Garrett's. He raised a fist to punch the air, then dropped low. He launched off his soft platform, falling into a roll as he landed. His momentum took him straight into the knees of a remnant, knocking the beast down.

Garrett punched it in the head, then slammed the edge of his hand on its throat. It struggled, eyes popping, only to have its face shattered by another blow. Garrett stood, grinning, as the remnant slowly drowned in its own blood.

Bette's horse wheeled to a stop beside him. She slid off, slapped the mare's rump and raised her fingers to her lips to let out a piercing whistle.

"Got it!" Mathias's call came from a distance, bellowed out over the sound of fighting.

Two remnant burst out from the press of bodies nearby and Bette and Garrett both lunged, Bette wielding her short sword and Garrett armed with a hefty knife he kept for backup.

"Where's yer sword?" Bette asked, twirling around to dodge a blow, then sticking the point of her weapon in the remnant's side.

"Bastian," Garrett grunted over the shoulder of his own target, as he rammed his knife in its belly.

Both remnant pulled back to strike again, despite the blood streaming to the ground.

"What?" she snapped. "He'll fall on it before he sticks it one of these beasties!"

Garrett lunged, then dove between a remnant's legs. He stabbed up with his knife, but lost his grip on the slippery, blood-coated hilt when the remnant collapsed. "Nay, Tansy's there ta make sure he doesn't do anythin' silly like that."

Bette swung her sword and spilled the guts of their last attacker. The remnant stared at the intestines tumbling out in a slippery mess, and for a moment, she wondered if he would keep fighting anyway.

She heaved a breath when he tumbled to the ground, dead. "How the bloody hell did ye walk into a mess like this?" she asked, her voice edged.

Around them, the fighting had died. She stared at the three remnant hanging from the trees, eyes bulging and faces black from the vines that strangled them.

"Druid can fight," Garrett muttered in awe next to her.

"Aye," she said. "But he's not got a thing on young Jakob. Did ye see what he did to those over there?" Bette pointed to where she had come in, and Garrett shook his head. "I think he exploded them."

"Drop anything from enough height, and it'll explode," a voice said over her shoulder, making her jump.

Bette turned around and socked Jakob in the gut. He protected himself with a sudden shield, his eyes turning black as he cast it, but still feigned the injury.

"Don't ye know not ta sneak up on a rearick after a fight, ye dickhead?" she asked, grinning.

"I do now!" he said.

"And you're welcome, by the way." She raised an expectant eyebrow to both men and waited. When neither said anything, she sighed. "Thank ye, Bette, fer runnin' to our rescue. Thank ye fer bailing us out when we got 'r empty ball sacks pinned ta the wall by a bunch of foul smellin' remnant. Thank ye fer skippin' yer lunch, even though it was steamin' pork belly roasted with clove and—"

"Stop, woman, yer makin' me stomach growl," Garrett said.

Bette shook her head in exasperation. "Un-fuckin'-believable," she muttered, stalking off to check that all her men were alive and all the remnant were not.

Jakob raised an eyebrow to Garrett. "Glad I'm not going home with her today," he said.

"I'd be cleanin' up before ye leave, or yer lass won't be glad you're there." Garrett pointed to Jakob's shirt, which, like Garrett's own, was soaked in congealing blood.

"I'll go wash down the river when we're done," Jakob said. Then, he paused. "Are we done?"

Garrett shook his head. "I've never seen that many remnant in one place, but I can't be offerin' a guarantee that there's no more o' the bastards lurkin' around."

"Garrett!" Bette's cry filtered through the babble of conversation.

He bent down, planting a boot on a dead remnant's leg as he plucked his knife from inside its thigh. He lifted it gingerly, wrinkling his nose at the bloody mess before wiping it on his shirt.

"Garrett!" Bette called again, impatience clear in her tone.

"I'm comin', lass." He picked his way over dead bodies, eyeing the wounded soldiers who sat in the few clear spaces, tending their wounds. He found Bette by the tree line, by a remnant lashed to a tree with thick vines.

"Rearick!" Mathias waved, grinning. "We caught a live one—and it looks like it might be a good one!"

Indeed, the trapped beast wore the bright scraps and layers clothes of the remnant leader—if remnant could be said to have a leader.

"Yer Chet?" Garrett asked.

Bette stood back, willing to let Garrett interrogate the creature.

"Chet!" the remnant bellowed. "Me Chet! Mighty Chet! Rip your face off, little man." Chet snarled, baring yellowed teeth.

"Mighty Chet look mighty fucked," Garrett said, laughing. "What're ye doin', ye stupid beast. The Madlands are that way."

"Chet from morning sun." He jerked his head east. "Seen remnant from late sun. They dumb."

"You're clearly smarter than them, though a bag of bricks would still give you a run for your money," Mathias said.

Chet frowned. "What?"

"I rest my case." Mathias's eyes flashed green, and the vines shifted, tightening enough to make Chet gasp for breath.

"What made ye come here?" Garrett asked.

"Monster. Chet kill monster! Chet strong! Chet kill you!"

"If ye killed it," Bette said, "Why'd ye leave?"

Chet pouted, mumbling. When Mathias gave him a warning glance and raised his arm, Chet spoke. "More monster. They come here. They kill you."

"What does this monster look like?" Garrett asked.

Chet spat at him. "Coward. Let go. Chet fight! Chet bite man face!"

"Aye, one of yer friends bit one of mine in his face. Ye wanna try?" Garrett got up close to Chet's face, and the remnant snapped his teeth, straining to get closer to the rearick. Garrett punched Chet in the gut and gave a satisfied grunt when the remnant coughed and wheezed.

"Chet kill you! Chet kill all you!" the remnant screamed when Garrett turned his back.

Garrett steeled his shoulders and took a breath, while Chet continued to threaten him. Then, he spun, arm out. His knife slipped between his fingers, shot through the air and planted itself between Chet's eyes.

"Yer a bloody whiner, Chet," Garrett grumbled, before plucking his weapon out of the remnant leader's skull. "Now, we'd best be checkin' the area fer more o' the remnant scum. Bastian!"

Garrett stomped through the mess of soldiers, bodies, and debris, looking for Bastian. He found Tansy first, leaning back against a broken section of wall.

"Where's yer lad?" he asked, irritably. The blood was starting to congeal on his clothes, sticking to his skin in a warm mess.

"Looking for Mathias," she said. "You would have walked straight past him."

"Ah, fuck," he said. He turned to go, but Tansy called him back.

"Do ye think this was all of 'em, Garrett?" Her face was smooth and seemed free of worry.

"Why?" he asked. "Do ye wanna come with us to find out?'

She grinned and nodded. "Bastian, too. I mean, he can't get into too much trouble with this many soldiers around him, right?"

Garrett scratched his chin, grimacing when his fingers dug a globbet of flesh out of his beard. "Aye. The lad needs the experience."

Tansy jumped to her feet excitedly and waved over Garrett's head. He turned to see Bastian heading their way.

The teeth marks and missing skin from his cheek had been healed, but crusted blood still smeared his face.

Bastian nodded at Garrett, then shivered. "Are we going home? It's getting cold. Really cold."

"That's just the battle rage wearin' off, lad!" Garrett slapped Bastian across the back hard enough to make him stumble. "We're off across the river. Can't leave until all the vermin are cleared, or ye'll have 'em breedin' and infestin' the forest again."

Bastian slumped tiredly. He looked to Tansy for support, but she shook her head.

"Uh uh," she said. "This is your circus, not mine. I'll tag along, but you have to see it through."

Bastian sucked in a breath, wavering on his feet as he looked around. "Tansy… there are piles of bodies here. Blood everywhere. Do you really think we can still save this?"

Garrett chuckled. "Wait for the rains ta come, lad. It'll clean up nice, and ye can knock down anythin' that doesn't."

Buoyed by Garrett's confidence, Bastian smiled. "Yeah. We can clean her up. Most of the walls need to come down anyway, and even if we re-use the stone, paint will cover the worst of it."

"That's me lad. Come on—let's roust the last of these fuckers out before it gets dark. I'd rather spend me night under a warm blanket with me lass than out here with the rats. Ye know, if ye touch her in just the right spot, her ears—"

"Garrett!" Bastian snapped, face as red as a beetroot. "Please, no more. Please? Bitch's oath, if Bette found out you were talking about—"

"If Bette found out ye were talkin' about what?" The rearick in question strode over, lips pursed and brow knitted as she glared at Garrett. "What lies are ye spreadin'?"

"Nothin, lass." Garrett grinned. "Just teasing the lad. He bites too easy to help it."

She shook her head, unconvinced. "Well, just to be safe, yer comin' with me, ye wee bastard." Bette waggled a finger at Garrett, and he followed her away, head dropped to his chest.

"Just scraped out of that," Bastian said, laughing nervously.

Bette called back over her shoulder. "Move yer ass, mystic! Ye comin'?"

"Fine! Fine, I'm coming." Bastian pulled himself to his feet and followed Bette as she barked orders to her men, ordering some to stay, and others to join the party going out to scour the remnant camp site.

Tansy nudged him with her shoulder. "I had fun today," she said.

He cocked an eyebrow at her grimy face and bloodied clothes. "I think you have remnant shit on your boot," he pointed out.

She grinned. "Sign of a good fight, that."

Bastian shook his head in disbelief. "I'm never going to be able to keep up with you. You know that, right?"

Tansy stopped walking, tugging on his sleeve to make him stop, too. "Bastian, I don't like you because you can fight—I mean, that's obvious." She rolled her eyes, and he cringed. "I like you because you're a nice person. And you're brave. You can't fight, and you still went toe to toe with some dirtbag, ballsack, rotfaced remnant because he tried to attack me."

"You saw that?" Bastian said, uncertainly. That particular fight hadn't exactly been a precision attack. In fact, he was pretty sure Garrett would have died laughing at Bastian's clumsy attempt to defend Tansy, even if the remnant had died in the end.

"Yeah, I saw." Tansy patted his arm. "I saw my friend put himself in harm's way to protect me. Awkwardly, sure. But you still did it, and that's braver than if Garrett or Mack or Jakob had done it."

Bastian shook his head. "Any of those guys would have taken that remnant out in one hit."

"Exactly!" Tansy exclaimed. "They wouldn't have been as eager to jump in if they weren't sure they'd win. You? You had a one in a million chance of surviving that, and you still didn't hesitate."

"Oh, come on," Bastian complained. "I know I'm bad, but a million? Give me better odds than that!"

"Ok," Tansy chuckled. "You *are* learning. And you're clumsy, but you know when to stand your ground. Maybe... one in a thousand?"

Bastian snorted and raised his eyes to the sky. "Why?" he asked the clouds. "Why me?"

"Because you're so damn fun to tease," Tansy said. She tugged his arm, and they set off with the troop again, now trailing at the back. "It's what I love most about you."

Heat prickled Bastian's face, and he ducked his head to hide it, wondering what she had really just meant to say.

They didn't speak after that, too busy trudging through damp brush and hilly terrain until they reached the remnant campsite. A couple of remnant had attacked the back of the party, but were easily dispatched before Tansy and Bastian could make their way through the soldiers to help.

The camp itself seemed deserted, so Garrett and Bette led the team over the shallow river. Bastian gripped Tansy's arm as he slipped and stumbled over the mossy rocks, while she laughed at his attempts to stay dry.

Two remnant jumped out of a tiny building. Tansy flicked her knife before Bastian could react. A moment later, both remnant lay on the dirt, dead eyes staring at the sky. Four knives had lodged in their skulls.

Tansy whistled. "How's that for a coordinated attack?" she said, plucking her knife and Garrett's both out of one skull, while Bette fetched hers and Jakob's.

"We make a good team, don't we?" Bette chuckled. "Good thing the lads have us here ta keep 'em safe."

Garrett grumbled something about keeping Bette safe in bed, but she didn't respond.

"Mack, Garrett and Jakob—search the buildings. Mathias? Where are ye?" Bette called. The druid jogged up to her. "Can ye send a bird to see if we've got any watchers?"

He nodded, and Bette proceeded to examine the cook fire. Charred animal bones littered the coals, and she poked them with a long stick.

Garrett emerged from one of the buildings, a long cobweb stuck between his beard and the doorway. "Nothin' here!" he called.

"Looks empty," Jakob confirmed.

"Mathias?" Bette probed.

"No remnant," the druid said, face drawn into a tight frown. "But there's something else…"

CHAPTER TWENTY-EIGHT

Marcus flew down the steps behind Aldred and burst out of the Temple doors. A line of guards, weapons at the ready, stood along the top of the path leading down to Craigston.

"Have you sent for your Master?" Marcus asked.

"Yes." Aldred spoke curtly, voice bouncing as he ran.

Travis, the guard who had raised the alarm when the battalion of heavily armed rearick had stormed over the ridge, clicked his heels.

"How did they get here so fast?" Aldred muttered.

"They took the back way," Marcus said. "Looking for us."

Marcus had spent the last forty minutes filling Aldred in on their trip back from Tahn. The odd adventure with the Arcadians hadn't seemed to bother the mystic, but his reaction to the events in Craigston had made him curse.

Aldred had responded with a story of the Master—or, Donna wearing Julianne's face—ordering a message be sent to the rearick, severing all of their treaties and trade agreements.

It had included a scathing line about the two rearick sent as hired guards, calling them useless and untrained, and, the line that caused the most pain, 'better use as carrion for the birds'.

Thinking that two of his guards were dead and that the Temple had broken faith, Tavich had barred passage through the town for any mystic, or for anyone returning from the Temple.

This had cut off trade, meaning that the mystics had no access to food they didn't already grow. Facing the impending winter had caused more than a little anxiety in the Temple, and the mystics had begun to turn on the false Julianne.

The ill feeling had culminated in Margit's death four days later. Deep in grief, most of the Temple residents had given up fighting against this cold new version of Julianne, one who wore her shields so tightly that even her most trusted advisors couldn't peek into her mind.

"Bastard rearick," Aldred said, then spat on the ground with disdain. "Treating our Master with such disrespect."

"After what Donna did to them?" Marcus asked.

Aldred dropped his eyes. "Bitch take me. This is a mess I don't know how we'll get out of."

Marcus shouldered his way through the line of Temple defenders. "Tavich?" he yelled.

A rearick clad head to toe in black armor stepped forwards. Two thick hands grasped his helmet and pulled it off. "You," Tavich sneered.

"Listen," Marcus said, pleading. "Your fight is not with us."

"No," Tavich snapped, and jutted his chin at the mystics. "It's with them. Stand aside, lad."

"No!" Marcus drew his sword, holding it high for the rearick army to see. He tossed it aside, letting it clatter and skid over the ice-covered rocks. "Your fight is with the New Dawn. Not Julianne and not the Temple."

"Julianne *is* the Temple, and the Temple is who our contracts were with!" Tavich cried. "The Temple is who tore them up and scattered the shreds at my feet. The Temple spat on the graves of our dead!"

Marcus jumped down the slope, coming face to face with the

man who led the army in front of him. Several rearick stepped forwards, hands on weapons. Two pulled swords and brandished them.

"You don't understand. You've been tricked!" Marcus spread his arms wide to show he was unarmed. "Donna is a mystic who went rogue. She got involved with a cult—that's why we crossed the Madlands with Bette and Garrett."

"Don't ye dare say their names!" A rearick spat from within the crowd. Muttering grew, and men shifted anxiously.

"They're my friends!" Marcus yelled. "And they are alive! I swear it on my mother's grave." He pointed back at the Temple. "Donna came back before us, and used her magic to mask herself as Julianne. *She's* the one who told you Bette and Garrett were dead. *She's* the one who ripped up treaties when she had no right to do so."

Aldred stepped forwards, his weapon pointed at the ground. "The boy speaks truth," he called. "I myself looked into Master Julianne's mind and saw it."

"She is a trickster!" Tavich called. "Like all of your kind! If she means to undo this mess, she should have stayed and faced trial, not run like a thief."

"You dare call me thief?" Julianne stood at the temple doors. Light bathed her, reflecting of pristine white robes and highlighting the barest shades of mahogany through her brown hair.

"I call ye how I see ye," Tavich growled, fist gripping his weapon tightly. "If ye wish to avoid war between our people, come with us."

"I will never leave my people," Julianne hissed. "Not to go with the likes of *you*."

Blood drained from Marcus's face as the men before him shuffled, standing low and ready for their next order.

"Stop!" Marcus darted back up the hill towards Julianne. "Just explain, Jules. Tell them about Donna."

Julianne shook her head. "They know. They choose not to

believe. Tavich has come here for war, not peace. It is war he shall have."

Julianne rose her staff into the air and brought the heel down against the rock she stood on. Her robe flapped and overhead, lightning struck from a clear sky. Mystic and rearick alike cowered, before some of the rearick growled and yelled, screaming "Fake!" and "Illusions!"

"Julianne?" Marcus cried from below. "What are you doing?"

Julianne spared him a cold glance. "I have done all I can. Using magic to force their compliance would stand against everything we have fought for."

"Julianne…" Something wasn't right. Certainty burrowed into Marcus's gut, and he took a step backwards.

"What's wrong?" A frown furrowed Julianne's brow and for a moment, he almost believed it was really her. "Aldred?" she called.

The guard approached, breaking formation to let another man scurry to take his place. "Yes, Master?"

"Do you think the rearick pose a genuine threat?"

Aldred shifted his gaze to the mass of stocky men barring their way down the path. "No arguing that, Master."

"If we fight… will we win?"

Aldred nodded reluctantly. "But if there is some way to keep the peace—"

"Would you give me over to them?" Julianne asked. "Or let them into the Temple to take our people captive? This is why we trained our fighters, Aldred. To defend."

"Aldred," Marcus said in a low voice. "It's—" Someone slammed into his shields, so hard and strong that he had no time to react. A presence ploughed through his mind, scattering his thoughts and sending his suspicions reeling.

"It's Donna," Marcus gasped. "She's in the Temple somewhere. I can feel her!"

Aldred looked to Julianne, fear and urgency in his face.

Julianne nodded. "Go, both of you. Find her! Perhaps then they will believe us."

Marcus raced into the Temple, Aldred hot on his heels.

CHAPTER TWENTY-NINE

Wake up.

Julianne groaned and tried to roll over, but her limbs were too heavy. She reached for the blanket, but something caught her wrist.

Wake up.

She slumped, brain refusing to kick into gear. She was uncomfortable—sore, even. If she just went back to sleep, maybe everything would stop hurting.

Oh, for bitch's sake, girl. WAKE UP!

Julianne's eyes shot open, and she sucked in a gasp of pain. She squeezed her eyes shut, then forced them back open. They slowly focused on the ropes binding her hands, the sling dangling uselessly across her chest.

"Oh, *fuck* that hurts," she whimpered.

"It's broken, of course it bloody well hurts," Margit snapped. She stooped down, slipping a small paring knife from her belt. "Stop complaining. Do you know I almost lost my toes, hiding out in that weather for four days?"

"Ow!" Julianne yelped as Margit cut through the bonds.

"Shh!" Margit hissed. "We don't know where that horrible woman is. Now, stay still while I block the pain from that arm."

"Margit, that's dangerous!" Julianne hissed.

"So is getting hit in the face by a psychopath," Margit said. "Have you seen inside that woman's head?" Margit clicked her tongue. "Of course, you couldn't. You never were good with broken minds."

"What are you talking about?" Julianne's head swam, but her pain faded as Margit's eyes shone white, blocking the sensors in Julianne's brain so she wouldn't feel her injury.

"That Donna is as broken as a shattered glass," Margit said. "Oh, her shields are strong enough, but a good mystic would be able to push past them... the problem was recognizing that it wasn't the shields causing the barrier."

"She finally snapped," Julianne whispered, her heart thudding a painful beat. "Rogan finally broke her."

Margit shrugged. "Someone did. But even a broken mind wouldn't wreak this much havoc if there weren't some nastiness deeper inside."

Julianne shook her head sadly. She didn't know Donna's whole story. Perhaps she really was just an innocent caught in a manipulators net, as unlikely as that seemed.

Margit pressed a knife into Julianne's hand. "The rearick are here," she said, urgency clipping her words short. "She's out there with them. Itching to start a war, that woman."

A smile crept over Julianne's face. "Perfect."

"What?" Margit squinted, then relaxed her face. "I see you're up to something. Something devious, no doubt... well, off with you then."

"Aren't you going to help?" Julianne asked.

Margit shook her head. "If I turn up now, that will just cause confusion. I did quite the job of pretending to be dead, you know." Her face lit up at the memory. "The funeral was wonderful, Julianne. And here I thought they all hated me!"

"Bullshit," Julianne said dryly. "You know we're all wrapped around your little finger, even if it is a bit arthritic these days."

Margit grinned. "Oh, Julianne. You'll make such a wonderful, cranky old bat one day."

"Not this day," Julianne replied, gathering her skirts with one hand. "I need to deliver a very stern message to one of my subjects."

Julianne trotted down the steps, ducking into a doorway when she heard footsteps around a corner. When two men passed, she grabbed one of their sleeves. "Marcus?" she asked.

Aldred reared back. "Master?"

"Yes, it's me. I know, Donna is outside." She gave Marcus a gentle shake. "You ok there, soldier?"

He looked at her with vacant eyes. "I have to find Donna," he said. "Julianne told me to."

"Fuck!" Julianne harnessed her magic, eyes turning white. "Aldred, help," she said.

The guardsman's eyes turned opaque to match hers. Julianne touched Marcus's shield. "Come on, Marcus," she whispered. "It's me."

Somewhere on the smooth wall surrounding his mind, a ripple trembled. She reached up to touch his face, and his defenses melted. "Follow me," she directed her helper.

Julianne was aware of Aldred's presence tailing her past Marcus's fallen shield. He had let Julianne in because he recognized her, not because she had forced through—she was still tired and needed to save her energy to address Donna.

Julianne flitted through Marcus's mind. As she touched memories, they flared to life, almost blinding her with the brightness and joy that he felt every moment. His love for her shone like a beacon, lighting her way through his mind.

Through the exuberant lightness, she noticed a tiny corner of darkness.

Donna, she thought, drifting towards it. Sure enough, a tendril of compulsion wrapped around a thought.

Aldred, here. She felt the guardsman join her and directed him towards the spell Donna had lodged in Marcus's mind. She watched as Aldred's magic reached out, gently tugging at the threads until it began to unravel.

The compulsion loosened. Then, with a shudder, it snapped back, cutting deeper into Marcus's mind.

Together, Julianne thought to her companion. Aldred started again, his patience soon rewarded by a loose end that unrolled to give them room to work. Julianne delicately unwound the spell, gripping it tightly when it tried to tighten again at the disturbance.

She held it out, threaded between prongs of magic, and raised it before Aldred. A glowing blade grew from his insubstantial form and sliced through the spell. It fell away, the scattered remains dissipating.

Julianne withdrew, staggering back to lean against the wall for support.

Marcus blinked slowly, and shook his head like a wet dog. "Jules?" he asked once he had steadied himself. "What are—oh, fuck me!"

"In the hallway?" Julianne asked. "I know I said mystics were open, Marcus, but that's a bit extreme even for us."

His ears turned fiery red as he ducked his face away from Aldred. "I didn't mean—I just… Oh, you're a bitch," he said.

Aldred raised an eyebrow at that. "I take it we are ready to proceed, Master?" he asked.

Julianne held up a finger, still slumped against the wall. Her eyes lit up again as she slipped into the deepest meditation she could manage without cutting herself off from her surroundings.

The men waited, Aldred patiently, Marcus less so. After a few minutes, Marcus whispered, "Jules? I hate to interrupt, but there's a real problem brewing out there."

"The rearick?" she asked, still staring with clouded eyes. "They can wait. As long as Donna doesn't get away this time."

Marcus didn't seem convinced, but leaned against the wall next to her, frowning as he drummed his fingers on the wall.

"That should do." Julianne pushed herself up, letting her eyes fade back to normal. She felt the sluggishness fall away. Though she was far from being at full strength, her lessons with Artemis forcing her to work through exhaustion and fatigue had conditioned her to working under such conditions.

Straightening her shoulders, Julianne strode outside, flanked by Marcus and Aldred. She didn't need to tell Marcus to tighten up his mental defenses—a quick prod at his shield showed it to be strong and steady.

She reached out to Aldred and brushed his shoulder. His shield relaxed enough to let her inside his head.

In a flurry of thoughts and impressions, she showed him how to create a looping shield between three anchor points. When she pulled in the third mystic, his face paled.

Margit? Aldred's stunned thought bounded through Julianne's head.

Oh, don't be an idiot, Aldred, Margit responded. *You don't think I'd really just die, do you? With the Temple in danger?*

Julianne felt Aldred bristle. *I buried you. I spoke at your funeral!*

And I appreciate it. Didn't know you had such a way with words, boy! Margit gave a mental chuckle.

"Blowed if I'm going to your next funeral," Aldred muttered aloud.

"What?" Marcus looked at him oddly, but Aldred just shook his head.

"Are we ready, gentlemen?" Julianne asked.

She strode through the door, flanked by the soldier and the guardsman. Cold wind whipped at her robes and streamed her hair across her face, but she ignored it.

Ahead, Donna stood atop a flat rock, her magic giving her Julianne's face and creating a halo of light around her.

"Showoff," Julianne said. Her eyes were sparkling white orbs, glowing in the dimming light of day. She lifted her head and called out, her voice laced with magic that made it echo in the minds of those who heard her call. "Traitor!"

The false Julianne spun on her rock, surprise etched on her features. Then, she laughed. "Imposter!" she yelled back.

A force slammed against Juliane's shield. Though it was buffered by Aldred and Margit, neither were trained in the art of holding a looping shield. The barrier shuddered under the force of Donna's attack.

Julianne fed her own power into the shield, steadying it. Beside her, a fat bolt of lightning smashed into the earth, shattering a nearby rock. Sparks flew from the stone, and the grass smoldered.

She let out a slow breath, steadying herself as the smoke cleared. The rock was still whole, smooth, unmarried by the stormy illusions.

Marcus jumped, his movement a blur in the corner of Julianne's eye. She turned her head to one side, just a little. He raised his sword, snarling at Donna.

More lightning, three bolts, one after the other, crashed down into the rearick army. They scattered, screaming as mind tricks made their armor burn.

Marcus staggered. He fell forward, catching himself before turning to Aldred. His eyes jerked to Donna, then back to Aldred.

"Fight it!" Julianne barked. "Fight!"

Marcus raised her a tortured glance, pain etched into his features. His sword raised.

Julianne drew back from her shield, enough to let it waver under Donna's brutal pressure. She used the remains of her power to slam into the other woman's mind, shoving against a shield far stronger than it should have been.

Marcus's sword flew down towards Aldred's neck, the guardsman's sweating face and closed eyes too distracted to notice.

At the last moment the sword twisted. Instead of cutting through Aldred's neck, the flat of the blade slammed into his shoulder. Aldred jerked back, and Julianne felt the joint shield crumble.

Marcus flung the sword, letting it slide, clattering down the rocks. He raised his hands, looking at them in horror before stumbling away.

Julianne's final defense, her last shields, crumbled.

Before Donna could force her way through, Julianne groped for a familiar presence, a mind to call to. She found it.

Now, she sent.

Donna flooded into her mind, raking at Julianne's immediate impressions. Pain scored her flesh, and she fell to her knees, writhing as Donna's magic inflicted sensations of burning agony on every one of her nerves.

Julianne screamed.

The pain stopped.

Donna's presence in her mind vanished.

Julianne lay on her back and sucked in a deep gasp. Above her, heavy grey clouds banked across the sky. A snowflake fell on her cheek, a tiny pinpoint of ice that quickly melted and dripped down her face.

"Jules!" Marcus scrambled to her, his face obscuring her view of the sky. "What the fuck?"

Julianne smiled. "I'm sorry," she said, voice weak.

"What?" Marcus slipped an arm under her and lifted, helping her to sit. "Julianne… what the fuck just happened?"

A wavering smile touched her face. "Tavich."

Marcus looked over his shoulder at the burly rearick leader stomping towards them, barely sparing a glance at the body sprawled on the snow, red hair splayed out around her.

Marcus reached for his scabbard, but Julianne put her hand over his.

"Julianne!" Tavich reached a hand out, and Julianne took it. With a swift jerk, he pulled her to her feet.

Legs still wobbling, she had to cling to Marcus to stay standing, but a giddy giggle escaped. "We did it," she said.

"Aye! Clever lass. Ye didn't have ta leave it til the last minute, though!" Tavich waved his finger at her, then chuckled. "But ye wouldn't be Selah's favorite if ye didn't have a touch o' the battle fever, would ye? Well played, lass."

"Uh, Tavich?" a rearick Julianne didn't recognize approached, eyes darting from his leader to the Mystic Master. "Are we not going to storm the Temple, then?"

"What?" Tavich's eyes bulged. "Don't be a dipshit, Carrup. Storm the Temple? Fucking rearick."

"But you said—"

Julianne interrupted smoothly. "I'm sorry, Carrup. Tavich and I worked out a plan, but it wasn't safe to tell anyone—anyone." Her eyes flicked to Marcus beseechingly. "Only Tavich and Margit knew."

"Margit?" Jonsen wandered over, his face dark. "Margit is dead. Isn't she?"

Julianne gave a polite cough.

"I was as surprised as you," Aldred said. He rolled his shoulder, then pulled back his robe to examine the black welt from Marcus's sword. He prodded it and winced.

"But... ah, Bastard's luck." Jonsen scowled. "She'd better not think she's getting another funeral like that one. Next time she dies, I'll box her up in cheap pine and toss it over the mountain." He wandered off, muttering about the cost of funerals.

"Sorry about the shoulder, Aldred." Marcus bowed his head apologetically.

"You couldn't help it," Julianne said. "I'm amazed you managed to turn the blade."

Marcus rubbed his head. "Is this what it's going to be like?" he asked. "Living here?"

"And you thought we were boring when you got here," Julianne chided. "Now, let's get this mess sorted out before my arm falls off."

CHAPTER THIRTY

Julianne relaxed into her thick pillows, the soothing warmth of a jug of elixir suffusing her body. Her fractured arm was splinted and bandaged and now rested on the blanket next to her, while Marcus sat at her other side, holding her good hand.

Sunlight filtered through the window, a crisp, cool light that did nothing to offset the frost speckling the edges of the window. Julianne shivered and turned her eyes towards the crackling fireplace.

"A prostitute." Across the room, Margit perched in a high-backed chair, shaking her head. "I wouldn't have believed *that* if I hadn't seen it in your head."

"I know," Julianne said. "But I'm glad he's happy."

"And this school?" Margit took a sip from the pewter mug in her hand. "You really think that Bastian has what it takes to undertake such a big project?"

Julianne nodded. "He was so young when we left," she mused. "But he's grown. We all have."

"Nothing stays the same forever," Marcus commented.

Margit's eyes flashed. "That's true. I'll wager you'll see some changes around here since our last little adventure." She snorted.

"My little trick seems to have put everyone in a snit. Do you know, Jonsen wouldn't even bring me dinner to my room last night?"

Julianne chuckled. "They'll come around. You did it to help keep the Temple safe, Margit."

After faking her death, the old woman had walked through early snow and treacherous darkness to slip past the Craigston orders and tip Tavich off about what was happening. They had kept Margit's information secret, to prevent Donna from realizing she had been found out.

"What was your plan, anyway?" Julianne asked. "I never did figure it out."

"Oh, she was showing all the signs of burnout," Margit said. "When we planned that so-called attack, we figured she would try and brain-wash the whole damn army to stop from being handed over."

"You were hoping she would magic herself to death?" Marcus asked.

Margit nodded. "Failing that, Tavich would have done what he did yesterday. There's no mind-magic that a swift knife to the gut won't stop."

Julianne blanched at the memory of Donna, convulsing on the hard stone as she died, blood spreading beneath her to stain the pristine snow.

Julianne briefly closed her eyes, and opened them when one of her guests rustled paper. When she looked, neither had moved.

"Did you hear that?" she asked. Marcus was just shaking his head when something scrabbled again, a skittering, mouse-like sound.

"Don't tell me those damn rats are back," Margit growled.

Julianne sat and swung her legs over the bed, eyes roaming the room.

Julianne?

Her heart stopped as she watched a bit of paper twirl on her desk.

Yes, Bastian? she replied distractedly.

You won't believe this. We found a portal! Or a door, I don't know. It's big and red and... things are coming out! Little armored creatures, with big front teeth and—

And glossy red skin? Julianne asked dryly. *Creatures that eat paper, and curl into a perfect ball when they're scared?*

Um... yes, actually. How did you...

Julianne watched the tiny beast scrabble at the desk, pointed nose twitching as it tried to find more paper. It came to the edge and tumbled off. Marcus snatched it from the air before it could strike the hard floor.

When he opened his hands, the small rock Julianne had carried with her all the way from Tahn was just that again—a rock. She tore a scrap of paper off the pile on her lap and reached out.

The rock trembled and slowly unfurled, snatching the paper from her fingers. The scrap wobbled as the little beast chewed it quickly.

"Well, that explains why it kept coming back after I left it behind," Julianne murmured. "And where all my papers went."

Master... Bastian sent the plea with all the awed confusion she felt herself. *What are they?*

I have no idea, Bastian. She reached out a finger and stroked the little animal's hard shell. *But I think... I think this is going to change everything.*

FINIS

Hi guys! Wow, what a whirlwind of a book! It was a little slower than expected in coming out, thanks to a crazy couple of months building, moving, and putting in some time helping out a few friends with various things. Still, I think it's the best in the series yet. Julianne, Marcus, Danil and the rearick are like old friends now, and having them around is easy. They know where the coffee cups are, and they know I don't like it when Danil leaves crumbs on the floor.

This is my birthday book. By the time you read this, I'll officially be 35. A pretty great age, actually. Too old to think drinking until vomiting is fun, too young for the arthritis to have fully set in yet. And always, ALWAYS young enough to dig at Michael for being older.

Next time I write one of these, I'll be doing it from my beautiful new house, on the shade of my verandah, listening to the chooks, the kookaburras and the babbling creek. I'll try get a sound bite of that for you to listen to. That way, if my next book takes three years, you'll know it's because I'm so relaxed, I'm asleep :D (I promise I won't actually do that. Probably.)

Goodbye for now, I'll see you all in two months or so. I can't wait to see what happens next!

First, THANK YOU for making it all the way to the back of the book, where the cool authors hang out…Or, at least one of us is cool, the other is 'older.'

I have a long memory Amy *(no, he doesn't)*, so you should be worried about the repercussions about sassing your elders. *(Seriously, I doubt Mike will think about his ten measly seconds after he finishes his Author Notes.)*

So, be worried. Be very worried indeed. *(He is such a liar! See notes above.)*

I'm 50, so I know all the crafty ways to get back at people. *(He doesn't know dick about getting back at people, plus he doesn't have a mean bone in his body, so don't worry.)*

I know I've mentioned it somewhere before, but if we could copy out some of Amy's comments in the Slack channel for the Age of Magic authors, she would have you in stitches. *(At least this is actually true.)*

Then again, her stuff makes ME blush. I presume it's the Aussie sense of humor and as an American, it's funny as hell, but my Puritan roots are showing.

(Whatever.)

If you want some interesting info on Amy, ask her HOW F#CKING FAST her builders are getting her house to go up. She showed us some pictures and I'm thinking, 'DAMN! You guys need to come to the US. You don't screw around.'

I've had three houses built in my life. The first one was back in 1999 and it started off great, then slowed… Then fast…Then slow again. If memory serves, it was a 2,900 square foot house (4 bedrooms) with one floor and took eight months.

Our second home was already six months completed, and took another three months so nine months in all.

Our third house, unfortunately, is in another country and will take at least two years. Don't add 'upgrades.' What it means here in America translates to 'push the house completion date back nine more months' in Cabo San Lucas.

I think it will be something like two and a half years minimum on that house. Possibly three years.

If we get it first quarter 2019.

On the plus side, we get free rooms at the resort every three months to so we can visit our dirt. The dirt is in a very pretty location, so that is nice. However, it's still just dirt.

As I mentioned above, I'm now fifty. So, I'm kinda feeling a kinship with the dirt with this whole age thing. *(He doesn't think he is old until he feels the bones creak when sitting in a position too long, or a backache when sitting Indian style on the floor to wrap presents.)*

Well, it's time I give you back your focus, so you can go and find the NEXT Kurtherian or Oriceran book to read ;-)

Ad Aeternitatem,

Michael Anderle

CONNECT WITH THE AUTHORS

Amy Hopkins Social
Website:
https://amyhopkinsauthor.com
Facebook:
https://www.facebook.com/thespellscribe

Connect with Michael Anderle

Website: http://lmbpn.com
Email List: http://lmbpn.com/email/

Social Media:

https://www.facebook.com/LMBPNPublishing
https://twitter.com/lmbpn
https://www.instagram.com/lmbpn_publishing/
https://www.bookbub.com/authors/michael-anderle